A COUNTESS TO REMEMBER

SHERRY EWING

KINGSBURG PRESS

DEDICATION

For Cathy W.

It's been a pleasure working with you at the day job for the past 14 years. I hope this dedication will bring you joy and make you smile. Thank you for your friendship and support over the years, my dear friend!

Kingsburg Pres
P.O. Box 475146
San Francisco, CA 94147
www.kingsburgpress.com

A Countess To Remember is a work of fiction. Names, characters, places, and incidents are a product of the author's imagination. Locales and public names are sometimes used for atmospheric purposes.

A Countess To Remember first appeared in *Desperate Daughters*, the 2022 box set by the Bluestocking Belles and friends. Each of us used some of the characters belonging to other authors in our stories. The participating authors have given me license to publish this story as a stand-alone with their characters included.

Editor: Jude Knight
Front Cover Design: Midnight Muse
Back Cover and Fonts: Sherry Ewing

A Countess To Remember/Sherry Ewing -- 1st ed.
ISBN eBook: 978-1-946177-66-7
ISBN Amazon Print: 978-1-946177-67-4
ISBN Expanded Distribution Print: 978-1-946177-68-1
Library of Congress Control Number: 2023900494

A Quest Through Time (Book Five)

Promises Made At Midnight: The Knights of Berwyck, A Quest Through Time (Book Six)

Regency

A Kiss for Charity: A de Courtenay Novella (Book One)

The Earl Takes A Wife: A de Courtenay Novella (Book Two)

Before I Found You: A de Courtenay Novella (Book Three)

Nothing But Time, A Family of Worth (Book One)

One Moment In Time: A Family of Worth (Book Two)

Under the Mistletoe

A Second Chance At Love

A Countess to Remember

Learn more about Sherry's books on her website at www.SherryEwing.com/books

Join Sherry's newsletter at http://bit.ly/2vGrqQM

A COUNTESS TO REMEMBER

CHAPTER 1

London, England
December, 1816

Richard, Viscount Cranfield peered out the window to the neat row of brick town houses before his carriage came to a stop at one that was familiar to him. He briefly leaned his head back upon the soft leather of the seat, dreading the confrontation he knew awaited him inside. He had been putting this off for months but he knew he couldn't delay the inevitable any longer.

Mrs. Penelope Lenox had been his mistress for the past several years. Unfortunately, Richard had been preoccupied with business matters of late, and he justified this excuse to not visit her more often at her town house. But it was more than just business that kept him away. Penelope had become increasingly possessive of his time, and she had made it perfectly clear she wanted more from him than he was able to give. She never mentioned that she was in love with him. Richard had his doubts she was even capable of such sentiment, and he certainly wasn't in love with his mistress.

His closest friends had warned him of what he himself hadn't seen at the time they had come to an understanding. She was an ambitious woman who had her sights on finding a gentleman who was not only rich but could also bring her a title. He should have listened to the men instead of attempting to convince them that their worries on his behalf were unfounded. He shook his head with the realization his friends had been right all along, and he had been the fool. He was tired of feeling as if he was nothing more than a financial means in order for her to have a better life. He needed to end their arrangement without further delay, hence his arrival to finish this once and for all.

The footman opened the door, let down the step and Richard left the carriage with a determined stride. He had barely knocked upon the front door when Penelope's butler welcomed him inside.

"Good to see you, my lord," Branson said taking his hat. "My lady is still upstairs."

Even though it was almost noon, Richard wasn't surprised the woman was still in bed. "No need to announce me, Branson. I can see myself up."

"Very well, sir. Should I send up refreshments?" he asked.

"Perhaps for your mistress but nothing for me. I won't be here long," Richard answered, before taking the steps up to the second floor. When he entered her bedroom after a brief knock, his mistress was quickly folding down the sheet covering her naked form just enough to expose the tops of her full breasts.

"Richard, darling. I wasn't expecting you today. I hope you can stay for an early dinner. I can have cook fix anything you desire." Penelope flashed an encouraging smile, patting the mattress next to her. Seductive brown eyes held a promise of what was in store for him if he but accepted her invitation.

He made his way across the room to sit in a chair near the fireplace. Her eyes followed his every move. "Not today, Penelope. I'm only here for a short visit."

"You look far too serious, darling, for this hour of the morning," she whispered. A worried frown marred her face.

"It's noon, my dear," Richard reminded her before taking out his pocket watch to note the time. He was going to be late for his next appointment, and keeping his parents waiting would result in a set down as though he was just out of the nursery. But there was no help for it. He was going to be late, and they would just have to wait.

"All the more reason for you to join me in bed," she purred. "We can entertain one another before having that early dinner."

His dark brow rose when she lowered the sheet

giving him a luscious glimpse of the bounty of her breasts before she once more covered herself with a laugh. The tease! She pushed her black hair away from her face. Those brown eyes twinkled in delight, thinking she had changed his mind. Her offer might have been tempting in the earlier years of their relationship, but she hadn't altered anything.

"We need to talk, Penelope," he replied seriously and watched when her face fell from her playful mood. "Perhaps you could put something on and join me here." Her eyes briefly flashed her disappointment when he motioned to the vacant chair across from him.

A nervous huff escaped her lips. Reluctantly, she left the bed naked, taking her time to stroll over to a nearby dressing screen in the corner of the room where a pink silk robe hung over the edge. She stretched as if to give Richard the extra opportunity to see her beautiful body and what he would be missing if he didn't take her up on his offer. She waited... as did he, knowing she wouldn't be changing his mind. With a heavy sigh, she pushed her arms into the garment and tied the sash around her waist. Her smile was seductive while her hips swayed when she gracefully walked toward him to sit in the chair. She crossed her legs, the robe opening to display her creamy skin. She positioned herself to show her body to its best advantage, a ploy she had used numerous times in their past.

But the action of her fingers drumming on the armrests of her chair gave away the true agitation she attempted to hide. She finally raised her brown eyes to his hazel ones. "Whatever do you wish to talk about, Richard?" She was nervous, and for good reason.

He raked his fingers through his brown hair with hints of blond highlights from the amount of time he spent outdoors. "I think you and I both know that our arrangement is no longer working for either of us," he began. She sputtered in anger.

"And whose fault is that?" she burst out, her fingers now gripping the arms of the chair, turning her knuckles white. "You barely come to see me anymore!"

"And we have had this conversation before. I cannot marry you. You knew this from the beginning yet still agreed you would be content to be only my mistress."

"I would be a good wife to you, Richard." Her comment only reaffirmed his decision to finally end their association.

She reached over to take a firm grip upon his arm. She was angry. He could see for himself the full effects of her displeasure, nor did he care for the look that crossed her features. "Don't be possessive, Penelope. It doesn't become you."

"But you promised me—"

"I promised you nothing other than to see that your financial needs were met in exchange for what you freely offered me," he replied. "But it's apparently long past the time that I settle our accounts, allowing you to find yourself another lover." His underlying tone conveyed he would not change his mind, yet still she pushed him further.

"You could dismiss me as easily as that?" she cried out in alarm.

"There is a reason I don't visit you as often as I used to, Penelope. If you stop to think about how our relationship has deteriorated over the past year, then you will realize you only have yourself to blame. You knew from the very beginning what would be between us was nothing more than a convenience. You agreed upon our terms. Yet you continue to ask more of me than I am able or willing to give. I will one day inherit my father's title of earl. For the last time, I cannot and will not ever be able to marry you."

His words were harsher than he intended. One look into her tormented brown eyes and he knew he had crushed whatever hopes she continued to have about becoming his wife.

"I just thought that perhaps with time..." her words dwindled away even as she blinked back the tears of the reality of what was never meant to be.

He reached out to brush one away with his thumb. "Unfortunately, nothing has changed from our original agreement, Penelope. I'm sorry if I have hurt you but you always knew the truth of the matter." Richard stood and headed toward the door.

"I wish I could change your mind," she whispered while she still held a margin of hope that they could remain together.

A previous conversation with his father echoed in his head when they had the never-ending talk about when Richard would finally wed. And his mother... if her son hadn't been their heir and they relied upon him to make a good match, she would have been throwing daggers in his direction. *Keep her as your mistress, if you must, but marry a title and a woman of worth*, his mother had all but ordered.

With thoughts of what his future held, Richard realized this would be the last time he would see Penelope. "It's well past time we went our separate ways, Penelope. I will settle your accounts and leave you enough to see you through the next six months."

A gasp escaped her before she composed herself into the strong woman he remembered when they first met. "That is more than generous. Thank you," she softly replied, nodding her head in agreement. She stood and made her way across the room. Standing on the tips of her toes, she kissed his cheek for the last time. "Goodbye, Richard."

He reached out to cup her cheek. "Goodbye, Penelope." He nodded, grateful she hadn't created a further scene.

Leaving her town house, he once more settled himself in his carriage, thankful Penelope took their parting relatively well. The driver put the horses into motion. Richard took another deep breath to prepare himself for his second conflict of the day, knowing a conversation with his parents seldom ended on a good note. Before long, the conveyance began to slow and he gazed out the window again to see another row of familiar town houses, one of them belonging to his parents. God only knew what awaited him inside, and he slowly walked up the steps to the brick structure in front of him. The door opened before he could even reach for the knob.

"Good afternoon, my lord," the butler said opening the portal wide.

"Good afternoon, Jenkins. How is Mrs. Jenkins?" Richard politely asked, as he handed over his hat and coat. The married couple had been in his parents' employ since Richard was a young man. How they remained loyal to their challenging employers was a mystery.

"Busy seeing to the household as always, my lord. The earl and countess are in the breakfast room, with Lady Josephine."

"No need to announce me, Jenkins. I know the way," Richard said repeating the words spoken to another butler earlier.

"As you wish, my lord," the butler nodded and left with his cloak and hat while Richard made his way through the town house.

He paid barely any attention to the opulent surroundings of one of several homes he had grown up in and would one day inherit. Luxury and wealth gleamed in abundance, a true testament to what his mother and father felt important in life. They cared for little else other than how others saw they lacked for nothing. Their summons had Richard guessing what could be so crucial, which is why he didn't care that he was running late. After all, they had been absent from most of his life and that of his sisters.

He made his way through the house to the breakfast room where the sun shone brightly through the floor to ceiling windows. He gave his parents a brief bow in greeting before smiling towards Josephine but her eyes portrayed her feelings all too well. What had they done to her now?

"You're late," his mother stated the obvious before taking a sip of her tea.

"You know how we hate to be kept waiting, son," his father said as he put down the newspaper he had been reading.

"But I am here now as you all but commanded." Richard took a seat next to Josephine who handed him a cup of tea. "How are you?"

"There is time later for the two of you to become reacquainted in this rare family reunion," his mother interrupted.

Richard nodded. "Very well, then. What exactly do you need from me this time?" he asked, not even making an attempt to hide his annoyance or remain polite.

His parents exchanged the briefest of glances before his father gave him his answer. "It's simple, Cranfield.

You are headed to York for their Season to ensure Josephine finds herself a suitable husband."

"What?" Richard roared while Josephine's cup rattled in the saucer. He looked over to his sibling while she silently mouthed the words *I'm sorry*.

His mother set her own cup down before she proceeded. "You'll have the whole staff of the York town house available for your convenience or feel free to take your own. I really don't care who runs the household. You know enough people in the *ton* that introductions won't be necessary once you arrive in York. Make the rounds, get invited to any balls or outings that may be occurring, or be seen at the races. You breed horses and have enough of them stabled there. The only thing that matters is that you get your sister engaged to be married. Heaven only knows how hard I've tried to find her a suitable match with no success in London."

"To men old enough to be my father," Josephine burst out.

"Silence!" their mother warned. "Every one of our selections would have seen you living in the lap of luxury. What more could you possibly want out of life?"

"How about love?" Richard and Josephine said in unison, and they exchanged a knowing smile between them.

Their father held up his hand before his wife could reply. Her red face more than amplified exactly how upset she truly was. "The two of you were always close, and the way you reply in unison is exactly why we are counting on you, Cranfield, to see the matter done. Maybe you can have better luck finding her a husband. At twenty-five years old she's already on the shelf and a spinster."

"Better Richard than what you've put before me," Josephine replied lifting her chin, but her false bravado dimmed when her chin quivered.

Their mother pointed a finger at her daughter. "You will keep a civil tongue, young lady, and remember we are still your parents!"

Richard reached over to take his sister's hand. "Since you've obviously washed your hands of this situation, then by all means, I will see to Josephine's needs including a proper chaperon to accompany us to York. Is there anything else you request of me?" he inquired, attempting to keep his voice calm when he was anything but. He wasn't angry at his sister since this was hardly her fault. But once again his parents proved they cared little for their well-being unless it elevated their social standings within the *ton*.

"Yes. Find your own lady to become your wife!" his mother exclaimed with a warning glare. "It's well past time you were also married."

And there it was... a grim reminder of his duties and the future that awaited him with some unknown woman.

Before Richard could reply, his father waved them off. "That will be enough. Your mother will see that the town house is open for your use in March. That should give you plenty enough time to settle whatever business you must attend to in London prior to your departure."

Richard stood, held out his hand to Josephine, and the two of them walked away from their parents. It wouldn't bother him in the least if he never laid eyes upon them again.

CHAPTER 2

Starbrook, England

Patience, Dowager Countess of Seahaven looked out the kitchen window to see the sun about to crest the horizon. The sight of the sky turning shades of pink and orange gave her an idea of how far behind she was as she continued kneading the dough in front of her. She had been in the kitchen for hours working by candlelight in order to get enough bread made in time for the loaves to be sent to the market to be sold. Another day in an endless set of days, or years actually, in which her family depended on each other to try and make ends meet. How blessed they were that they'd kept from Society the fact they worked at various skills to bring income into the household. Some days, she was glad there was enough food to even feed her own large family.

SHERRY EWING

Sectioning off the dough and forming it into multiple balls, she placed each one in a separate bowl, put a cloth over the top to let it rise, and cleaned off the countertop before she finally took a moment to sit down. Her tea had grown cold, but she was too tired to reheat it or make another cup. She took a sip, enjoying the rare bit of solitude that only this hour of the morning could bring.

Patience gave a weary sigh as the burden of her responsibility for all her stepdaughters, along with her own precious Jane, who was only three years of age, came crashing down upon her. She always tried to put on a brave front for everyone's sake, including her own, but she doubted she fooled her family, and she certainly didn't fool herself. They needed to scrape up enough money in order to see the oldest daughters wed but how could they ever afford a Season in London? It just couldn't be done.

She finished her tea and rose from her seat to head upstairs to her room to change since she had time before she would need to get the bread formed and into the oven. She tried to ignore the shabby cottage she lived in. Although neat and clean, the place was hardly befitting a countess. Most would expect to find her living in a lovely town house in London. But life was unfair, and Patience had come to realize that she had to depend on herself and those stepdaughters who were old enough to bring in whatever money they could from various trades.

Upon her husband's death, the new earl, who was a distant cousin, and his wife had given Patience a small amount due to her from her husband's will and turned her out. The will had appointed her as the custodial guardian of her husband's daughters from his previous marriages. Some of them were actually older than herself. The new earl had shared out a modest sum as a dowry, but it was a pittance once divided among all the daughters and wouldn't be available until after they wed.

Patience could dredge up the day when she had sat in the study once belonging to her husband while the new earl and his wife argued about the sum. She had a moment of pity for the man but it was short lived. His wife controlled him, and Patience could still remember the gleam of satisfaction in the woman's eyes when she had won the argument... the man was a spineless fool! Patience had left what once had been her home with her stepdaughters and Jane, and never looked back. She'd been given no other choice on the matter.

The last stair creaked despite her attempt to remain quiet so as not to awaken the household, and she made her way down the hallway to her room before soundlessly closing the door. Opening the drapes to let in the morning light, she went to sit at her vanity and stared at the reflection in the mirror. Her strawberry blonde hair had been swept up in a bun to keep the tresses off her face while in the kitchen, but it was the shadows beneath her blue-grey eyes that worried her. She was beyond exhausted, and it showed. She pinched her cheeks to bring color to them, hoping this would help, and quickly redid her hair for the day before heading to a wardrobe to pick out a gown. She was used to dressing herself; they all were. They could barely afford the housekeeper and nursemaid who followed her when they were turned out from Seahaven, let alone additional staff.

Who would have ever thought that, at the age of only twenty-two, she would not only be a widow but a dowager countess at that? *Dowager!* she thought in disgust. A frown formed on her brows while she dressed. She had always associated that word with a woman of older years, not someone who was yet so young.

Despite not wishing to relive unpleasantries, her thoughts still went to the day Henry Reginald Bigglesworth, Earl of Seahaven, had shown up at her parent's home... this very cottage, in fact. Although still a handsome man, he had been old enough to be her father, or grandfather for that matter. His proposal of marriage meant Patience would become a countess and would want for nothing, which was appealing, of course. Patience finally agreed to the marriage in order to help her parents.

Harold and Emily Egerton were far from the realm of high Society and had sold baked goods to a small bakery in Starbrook. Her mother had fallen out with her own family when she married beneath her station in life. They claimed she had disgraced the St. Aubyn name. Her mother had always told Patience that, when love found you, you needed to grasp hold of it and never let go. Not that love had anything to do with her decision to marry Henry. This had been a once in a lifetime opportunity to become elevated back into the *ton* that her mother had left behind, or so they had convinced their daughter.

She and the earl wed quietly in the village chapel in the spring of 1813 when Patience had barely turned eighteen. But her wedding was the first time she had glimpsed the faces of all his daughters sitting in the first two pews of the church. Nine girls ranging from older than her to two little girls. The reality that she would be his fifth wife hit her. She had quietly said her vows all the while thinking she was apparently his last chance at siring a son to carry on his name and title.

Eight months after their wedding, Henry passed away from some unknown ailment. Two months later, she gave birth to Jane. Henry would have been disappointed at siring yet another daughter. But fate, or perhaps God, wasn't done creating further catastrophe in Patience's young life. Her parents had come to Seahaven to support Patience through Jane's birth. They were returning home two weeks afterwards when a thunderstorm came up out of nowhere, and the driver lost control of the team on a narrow stretch of road. The carriage overturned and fell over into a steep ravine. No one survived. Tears threatened to well up in her eyes as she relived the memory. She had never felt more alone than she had from their loss. But God surely felt her shoulders were strong enough to bear the burden of this latest twist, including the responsibility of a household of stepdaughters left in her care.

Patience inherited her family home, although, without her parents' presence, the cottage seemed to lack some of the warmth that used to fill each room. The place needed more repairs than she and her stepdaughters could afford and was located outside of the small village of Starbrook. Their cottage was as different as it could be from her old home of Seahaven and thankfully was far enough away that the family never saw the new earl and his countess. Almost all of her stepdaughters also resided with her.

She shook off her sudden melancholy mood, lifted her chin and left her room to check on the youngest children in the bedroom next to her own. Quietly opening the door, she saw that Jane was still asleep in her crib. Emma who was twelve and Merrilyn age ten, from her husband's fourth marriage, also still slept in their separate beds. She closed the door and turned, almost running straight into the nursemaid, Hannah.

"M-my apologies, m-my l-lady," Hannah stammered softly as she righted herself along with the linens she balanced in her arms.

"The fault was mine, Hannah. You've done nothing wrong," Patience replied before grabbing one of the linens about to fall. She'd been so grateful Hannah continued to stay with them and accepted such a small amount for her services to the family. But Hannah had told Patience when they left Seahaven that she was committed to Emma and Merrilyn and would follow the girls wherever they may live. She had been more than happy when Jane was born, giving her another young child to care for.

Hannah nodded to the door. "The little misses are still asleep?" she asked, and Patience nodded. "I'll check on them later and change their bedding once they're up."

"Thank you, Hannah. I don't know what I'd do without you," Patience replied before heading toward the stairs. She met Barbara coming out of her own bedroom, and the two women descended and made their way to the kitchen. Barbara was from her husband's second marriage and was a music teacher.

Patience put a kettle of water on the stove before taking out several containers to put her bread in now that it had risen enough.

"You were up early, Patience," Barbara mentioned as she reached for a tin of loose-leaf tea and several cups. Patience smiled at the young woman, who was the second eldest of all the sisters and five years older than Patience.

"The bread won't bake itself," Patience replied as she lined up the pans. She was thankful she had been able to continue the same arrangement to sell her baked goods that her parents had had with the local bakery.

"You could have woken me to help." her step-daughter said stifling a yawn.

"No, I couldn't, not when I know you have a full day teaching lessons in the village. You know I always manage."

Barbara sighed. "I know, but I still worry how we will continue to survive."

Patience gripped the edges of the counter, her knuckles turning white while she kept her head lowered. *I will not cry... I will not cry...* "As do I," she at last managed to whisper before going back to the task at hand. If she didn't get these loaves into the oven, they'd miss out on the extra money they so desperately needed.

The two women were silent as they began the chore of preparing breakfast for the family that had as yet come down to join them. A knock on the front door sounded in the distance, and Patience and Barbara exchanged a look between them.

"Who could that be at this hour?" Barbara asked causing Patience to shrug.

They didn't have long to wait before the house-keeper, Mrs. Crewe, came into the kitchen with a note held in her hands bringing it to Patience.

"This just arrived by special messenger, my lady," she said handing over the letter.

"Thank you, Mrs. Crewe." Patience exclaimed, once more thankful for another servant who refused to leave her employer. The woman left, and Patience went to sit at the kitchen table, breaking the wax seal. A shiny brass key fell onto the table.

She picked it up with a fair amount of curiosity. Patience began to read, her eyes widening at what the letter revealed. "We're saved," she exclaimed before handing the letter over to Barbara to read.

"Who is Rose?" Barbara asked after skimming the contents.

"Lady Rose St. Aubyn is a cousin on my mother's side of the family. She is the only child of a St. Aubyn earl, inherited his money when he passed away, and never married. While she is traveling in the East, she's invited us to live rent free in her town house in York. Can you believe it, Barbara? This can't come at a better time. We can be there when the York Season begins. We just might be able to find husbands for Josefina and the twins, Ivy and Iris!" These three stepdaughters were from Henry's third marriage, Josefina being the oldest at nineteen and Ivy and Iris aged eighteen.

"Will we still be able to afford a Season for the girls, especially after how much we spent on presents for Christmas next week? With almost everyone coming home for the holiday, our expenses will certainly be higher than they normally are," Barbara asked, worry etched upon her brow.

Patience looked up from her excitement to briefly ponder the matter. "An opportunity like this won't come again but I see your point." She read the letter again. "The town house is available for the next six months.

We might be able to manage six or seven weeks at the height of the Season. We'd have to swap dresses and trims, maybe even dyeing them and exchanging accessories. We need to have a meeting... all of us, say by Twelfth Night since Rose would like a reply as soon as possible. Perhaps you can see if Josefina is up and she can accompany me to Harrogate when I drop off the bread. I'd like her to go to confirm with Dorothea that she can make it home for Christmas. I won't have time to stop in the hotel where she's working beforehand to ask her myself, and I know how busy Doro's been with running the catering business."

"I'll check to see if Josefina is awake," Barbara said, before going to the stove, taking the kettle, and pouring two cups of tea. "Can you manage breakfast alone or should I send one of the other girls to help you?"

"I can manage but thank you," Patience said, waving her off. Barbara took her tea with her and hurried from the room.

Patience got to work on the bread and smiled. She could not even remember the last time that she had been so hopeful. She was excited for all the possibilities that awaited them in the months to come.

CHAPTER 3

Whites, London

Richard entered his club for a much-needed respite from his parents, who continued to plague him even after two weeks of living under their roof. One would think that once he agreed to see Josephine settled in York for the Season, then that would have been the end of their harping. But, no. They continued their assault to ensure every detail for Josephine had been arranged and also argued he needed to wed within the year.

He had stayed through the holidays to ring in the new year so his sister would have moral support but he apologized when he couldn't stand being under the same roof any longer. He promised her he would see that they were settled into the York town house as soon as possible. As far as Josephine was concerned, the move couldn't happen soon enough.

Handing his hat and coat to the doorman, Richard entered the lounge and saw a far table already occupied by the close friends with whom he had attended Oxford. Frederick Maddox and Digby Osgood were the married men of the bunch, both busy with raising their families together with the lovely women they had wed. That left himself, Milton Sutton, and George Chadwick as the bachelors of the group. Digby raised a hand to a passing servant and, by the time Richard stopped at several tables to say hello to other acquaintances, a drink was ready for him when he arrived to greet his friends.

"Gentlemen," Richard said, taking a seat and reaching for the brandy. "It's been too long."

"Some of us have been enjoying wedded bliss," Frederick announced with a nod to Digby who smiled in agreement. "The three of you should try it."

"Good heavens, why?" George asked adjusting the cufflink at his wrist, not that anything was ever out of place with his wardrobe.

Digby chuckled. "You may find that you enjoy it."

Milton grimaced. "I'd rather pay for the upkeep on a mistress than have a wife harping at me every moment of my life." He gave Richard an odd sideways glance and cleared his throat. "I have yet to find a woman agreeable enough to marry."

Richard took a sip of his drink before setting it

down on the table. "We can't all be so lucky as to find such lovely women as Margaret and Constance to spend our lives with." There was a round of agreements before Richard continued. "Speaking of mistresses... I let Penelope go last month. Should have done it sooner, but she's well taken care of until she can find another man to see to her needs."

Frederick's brow rose and a knowing smirk stretched across his lips. "I told you—"

"—don't you dare finish that thought," Richard warned.

Milton took up his drink with a knowing smirk. "From what you've told us, I'm surprised you didn't let her go sooner. You would think our mistresses would remember that if and when we marry we would need to find a suitable woman—"

"—and not someone of their ilk," George muttered.

"Don't be a snob, Georgie," Digby said with a warning glare. "They cannot help that they've fallen on hard times and must do what they can to survive. I highly doubt any woman just wakes up one morning and decides to ruin her reputation and have a man support her without marriage."

Richard remained silent for several minutes remembering how he had felt when he dashed Penelope's unfounded hopes. But that was now over, and he needed to move on with his life just as she did.

"In any case, I am traveling another road in life at the moment as I've been given the task of seeing to a

Season to find Josephine a suitable husband," Richard said looking at the men before him.

Milton choked on his drink.

Frederick slapped him on the back. "She is still unwed?' he asked, his brow raised with his question.

"Apparently my parents think a man with one foot in the grave would make my sister a suitable husband. She thinks otherwise, and I agree. Josephine shouldn't have to marry some old codger just because he has plenty of money, and that's what's important in the eyes of my mother and father."

Frederick nodded in agreement. "Lady Josephine was always a lovely young woman. Margaret has told me a number of times any man would be lucky to call her his wife."

Digby sat back in his chair with a smirk. "Which reminds me that the three of you should be very careful."

Richard, Milton, and George all turned their attention to the two married men in their group.

"Should I ask why?" Richard murmured with a worried frown.

Frederick gave them a wicked grin. "Because my Margaret and Digby's Constance are ready to throw eligible ladies in your direction if you don't find yourself a lady of your choice to wed. They've made it their mission to end your days of being bachelors."

"Eh gads!" George groaned. "Tell them to leave me out of their plans.

Milton only took up his drink again, swirling the amber liquid in the crystal glass.

Richard shuddered before pinching the bridge of his nose at the thought of the two women throwing marriageable young ladies in his direction... no matter how well intended. "I cannot begin to tell you how much I do not need them meddling in my life."

Digby shrugged. "You know our wives. They just want you to be as happy as we are. They'd go to the end of the earth to make it happen."

"Then you and your wives will have to follow me to York, for that is my destination," Richard replied relaxing back in his chair.

"Why York?" Frederick inquired, before reaching for his glass. Finding it empty, he motioned to a passing servant to see the glass filled again.

"My family has a town house there. The earl and countess feel that Josephine has run her chances with any eligible men with a title here in London." Richard's low tone conveyed his underlying anger at the situation.

Frederick shook his head. "I could never understand your parents, Richard. You do yourself and your sister proud to remove her from their influence."

"York, you say?" Milton asked gazing at Richard who nodded. "I was thinking of attending the horse races they have there in May. Maybe I'll open my town house for the Season and join you."

Richard chuckled. "The more the merrier, and I could use the reinforcements. Not that Josephine is a problem. I'd do anything for my sister, and if it annoys my mother and father in the process, then that's a bonus."

The men laughed and clinked their glasses together as Richard began telling them more details of when he would depart. When he finally left White's, there was a new entry in the betting book about the estimated date on when Richard, Viscount Cranfield would find himself hitched and to whom.

CHAPTER 4

Twelfth Night
January 6th, 1817

Patience pulled the blanket over Jane, smoothed down her curly auburn hair and quietly left the nursery, knowing Hannah would check on her later before she, too, retired for the night. Her hand slid along the well-worn oak banister as she went half way up the second set of stairs to softly call out to Elizabeth, or Bess as she preferred, who was working in the attic.

"Bess... are you coming?" Patience asked, somewhat impatiently, knowing nearly everyone else was already in the sitting room.

"Yes. I'll be right there," Bess replied, but Patience knew her eldest stepdaughter, age thirty and the only daughter from her husband's first wife, would no doubt get lost while translating Egyptian hieroglyphics. If she didn't join them in the next few minutes then their meeting would have to go on without her.

As she was about to descend the stairs, Barbara and the twins, who giggled among themselves, joined her. She shared a knowing look at Barbara, who smiled at the possibilities for the girls if only they could scrape up enough money to make this work.

They made their way to the front sitting room where her stepdaughters went to sit in various places around the tidy but tattered room. Josefina was already seated near the hearth while Doro sat at a large desk that had seen better days, much like the rest of the room. Once again, Patience was reminded how different the cottage was to their past life at Seahaven where every luxury had been afforded them.

"Why are we all here?" Ivy and Iris asked at the same time, before they exchanged a look.

"Be patient, girls," Patience suggested, although it was hard to hide her own excitement.

Josefina looked around at her sisters. "Won't Bess be joining us?"

Patience looked toward the entrance to the room, but there was still no sign of her eldest stepdaughter. Doro stopped what she was doing but, at a short nod from Patience, continued her work. "We'll begin without her if she's not here by the time Doro finishes."

Patience made her way toward the desk to look over Doro's shoulder, although she tried not to hover. Doro drew a line at the bottom of the column of figures and began to add them up. Her nerves getting the better of her, Patience began to pace the silent room while her six stepdaughters watched Doro's movements with the quill. She continued moving up and down the page, jotting a figure down and then beginning again at the top. Gazing at all the women in the room, there was no mistaking the strong family resemblance identifying them all as sisters. Practically the same height, they each had that straight nose and determined Bigglesworth chin.

Doro finished adding up their expenses, wrote down the last figure and sat back in her chair. She looked around the room as all the women held their breath in anticipation of her news.

Barbara broke the silence of the room. "Well, Doro? Do we have enough?"

"Barely," she replied. "We'll have to make economies."

Barbara shrugged. "We've been making economies for the past four years. That won't change whether we remain here or are visiting York."

Ivy sat up straight in her chair. "York? We may be going to York?"

"To give Josefina, Iris and you a season. If it can be done financially." Susana interrupted. She was the dressmaker in the family. At the age of twenty-five, she was also from Henry's second marriage and so Barbara and Doro's full sister.

Josefina, Iris and Ivy all gasped in startled surprise.

Doro turned her attention to her stepmother, who had yet to express an opinion. "What do you say, Patience? You are the one we will need to sponsor the girls. And it's your cousin Rose who owns the town house."

Barbara frowned. "I could stay here at Starbrook with the little ones, if that would help."

Patience raised her eyes in gratitude for Barbara's thoughtfulness. "Oh, no. I couldn't do this without you, dear one. Besides, the younger children may as well join us so we don't have the expense of running two households at the same time. I think we should proceed with taking my cousin up on her generous offer. I propose we move to the town house at the end of March, which will give us time between now and then to figure out any of the details I'm certain we're missing. I believe this is the best chance for your sisters, for all of us, really. Imagine if one of them makes a magnificent match."

Josefina, Iris and Ivy clapped their hands in glee, moved their chairs closer together, and began whispering among themselves.

Doro glanced among the women in the room. "The earl made it clear we can split the dowry trust as we see fit. Divided among all of us, it's a pittance. If we put the money all on Iris, Ivy, and Josefina—"

"—but Doro what about the rest of you," Ivy shouted out, in concern for her sisters.

"Don't interrupt, Ivy. Be sensible," Doro warned

before continuing. "If we do this, we may just have enough for the three of you to snag a suitor. It benefits all of us to do so."

"If they find a husband who is kind and respectful, I shall be satisfied," Susana said. "If you think we can manage it, I believe we must try."

Patience came over to her and rested her hand upon her shoulder. "We would be relying on you to dye dresses and any other accessories so none of the girls would be wearing the same gown in the same week," she said thinking of the time and energy that would be needed to make this work.

Susana smiled before taking up the knitting she had left in her lap. "Don't worry. I can manage."

"Waiting does not make financial sense," Doro said, obviously still concerned with expenses. "Since Patience has been offered her cousin's town house for the Season, this will save us on expenses of running the cottage."

Patience nodded in agreement. "The only problem I foresee is we will still be without servants, as Rose stated she would be giving them a much-needed holiday. But I'm certain we can convince Mrs. Crewe to run the York town house and Hannah will be more than willing to look after the younger children. I have no idea, however, what we'll do for a butler. It might appear questionable for us to be answering our own door." Patience gave a heavy sigh as the logistics of a move began to overwhelm her. She finally quit her pacing and took a seat, picking up a garment with tiny rosebuds she had recently been working on.

"We can figure out the rest in the coming months," said Barbara. "I agree we should take the chance and go to York, including the little ones. With the cottage empty, we could rent it out, which will help us to fund the Season. Between us, we have earned enough to manage without working while we're there, though I suppose some of us could continue some of our enter-prises in York."

Patience put down her embroidering. "Oh no, Barbara. We must never let anyone in Society know we work for our bread." She took a moment to look at each one of her stepdaughters. "This is very important, my dearest ones. We will be trading on your father's title, and must appear to be, if not wealthy, then at least solvent."

"We are solvent," Barbara replied, "because I teach piano, Doro has been managing a catering business, Susana makes the finest hats in fifty miles, you and Doro are wonderful bakers, Josefina sells her medical herbs, and Ivy and Iris are superb artists selling their trinkets."

"That is quite true, and I cannot express my grati-tude to each and every one of you for what you've contributed to the household to keep this roof over our heads. I couldn't have done this without your help. But we must forget everything we've been doing to survive if we are to make a success of this enterprise." Patience picked up the letter from her cousin. "We can have the house until the Season is over in mid-May."

Barbara put down her own knitting and crossed to give Patience a kiss on her cheek. "We have a great deal to do, Patience." She went over to the desk, picked up a notepad and a pencil, and returned to her chair. "We had better start making lists."

Patience nodded her head in agreement and was momentarily lost in thought regarding Bess who remained upstairs. She would need to find some way to entice her bluestocking eldest to put aside her translations in favor of teas and receptions... no easy task. Returning to the present, Patience smiled in gratitude to her stepdaughters, who continued to all pull together to help one another out. She couldn't have survived without each of them. She was truly blessed.

CHAPTER 5

York, England
March 28th, 1817

R ichard stared at his reflection in the mirror
while he finished buttoning the beige waistcoat
with embroidered flowers. His cravat was tied in an
intricate knot and a ruby stick pin winked from the
folds. Dark brown trousers hugged his muscular thighs
while his boots gleamed from the sunlight reflecting
through his bedroom window. His valet, Owen, held a
matching coat ready for him that would complete his
look for the day. The waistcoat had been a gift from his
sister, and while the flowers were a bit much for his
regular taste, he knew it would please her to see him
wearing the garment.

Thus, when he pulled his arms through the sleeves
of his coat and the garment settled on broad shoulders,

he was ready for the onslaught of what his responsibilities entailed. Getting his sister engaged was his first priority. Finding a suitable wife was second on his agenda. He wasn't in the least bit hopeful he'd find someone whom he could one day call his wife in the short amount of time they would be in York. Better to focus on Josephine. She was all that mattered, so she wouldn't have to live under their parent's roof.

Owen smoothed the shoulder of the coat as though removing some unseen speck of lint.

"Will I do, Owen?" Richard inquired in amusement. He was well aware his valet would never allow his master to go out into the world looking anything but his very best.

"Yes, my lord. You will do very nicely, indeed," he said, before handing Richard his hat.

With a brief nod, Richard left the master bedroom in the town house he would now call home for the next couple of months. Josephine was waiting for him at the foot of the stairs, donning her gloves. She looked lovely in a light blue muslin gown with a darker blue ribbon tied in a fashionable bow at her back. The neckline and hem were embroidered in an intricate pattern and her bonnet with white lace at the rim framed her face. A few wisps of her blonde hair with darker highlights escaped her coiffure and curled pleasingly at her cheeks. She was like a breath of fresh air, and if the gentlemen in York didn't become smitten with her upon first sight, then they were all fools.

"Good afternoon, Richard," she said brightly, as she came over to kiss his cheek when he bent down. "It's a lovely day for a carriage ride."

"The sun will shine all the brighter to have my beautiful sister sitting beside me," he complimented her before placing her hand in the crook of his arm. "Are you ready to be *seen*, my dear?"

A groan escaped her when she halted their steps into the entrance hall. She playfully swatted his arm. "Please don't ruin the day with comments like that, brother. It's barely even noon! You make me feel as if I'm about to be auctioned off at the market."

"That wasn't my intention, Josephine. You know I only have your best interest at heart. Remember why we are here in York, and that's to find you a husband—"

"—and you a wife," she finished tossing him a smug look.

"Eh gads, don't start on that Josephine, or you'll start sounding like mother."

"Don't you dare compare me to her," she cried out in alarm, and Richard felt horrible that such words had tumbled from his mouth.

He gave his sister a reassuring hug before leading her to the entrance door. "Please forgive me, dearest Josephine. Apparently I am doomed to allow my tongue to get the better of me today. You can remind me how obnoxious I become as the day progresses." Richard escorted her through the door.

Their open carriage waited for them in front of

A COUNTESS TO REMEMBER

their residence, and as Josephine strode across the paved walk to the road, she shielded her eyes to peer down the street. "Oh look, Richard. It appears as though someone is moving in several doors down. Isn't that where Rose St Aubyn lives when she is not travelling around the world?" Josephine had been fascinated by the York housekeeper's stories of their enterprising neighbor.

"Perhaps she has let her house. Isn't that Lady Elizabeth Bigglesworth coming out of the door?" Richard asked, following his sister's gaze as a carriage left and another pulled up to the walkway. The lady at the door greeted several ladies heading toward the town house while the door to the next carriage opened. Another woman descended, followed by two younger girls.

"Yes, I think so. Remember, we met her years ago when you brought me up to York? You were here for the races, and so was their father, and he introduced you to her after church one day. I believe she likes to go by Lady Bess. Yes, it must be her, because that's her stepsister Lady Barbara getting out of the carriage. I met her when my governess took me to tea at the Seahaven town house. Those must be her younger stepsisters, though they have grown up since I met them five years ago. Have you met her, Richard?" She looked upon him as though she was about to play matchmaker.

"I haven't had the pleasure of being introduced to Lady Barbara but, whatever you are thinking, the answer is no," he warned, but Josephine was in a world of her own and wasn't listening to a word he was saying.

"Let me introduce you," she replied instead, tugging on his arm.

"This is hardly appropriate."

"Nonsense, Richard, don't be such a bore. They'll obviously be our neighbors, after all," she said brightly, and in order not to cause a scene on the street, Richard found himself escorting his sister to meet the lady.

Introductions were made while the two younger girls chatted about how excited they were to be here in York. Their elder sister made several attempts to calm them without much success before she turned her attention to the carriage, where a woman was attempting to hand a wiggling toddler to Lady Barbara.

"Let me take her," the lady exclaimed, as a nurse-maid came from the household to usher the younger children inside.

The unseen woman was still in the carriage, as if she was still preparing to collect whatever had been left behind. A small dainty shoe poked out onto the edge of the step and Richard heard her heavy sigh that she made no attempt to mask.

Richard stepped forward, offering his hand. "May I be of assistance, my lady?"

"You are most kind," the lady inside said. She put her hand in his and Richard swore he felt a tingling sensation rush up his arm.

"Where are my manners?" Lady Barbara exclaimed.

"May I introduce my stepmother, Patience, Lady Seahaven. Patience, this is Lord Cranfield and his sister Lady Josephine."

Richard was prepared for a matronly woman to reveal herself as she alit from the carriage. But when she lifted her head once upon solid ground to acknowledge their introductions, he was unprepared for the young beauty he faced. Blue-grey eyes that could rival the sky above met his. Wisps of strawberry blonde hair had escaped her bonnet while her porcelain skin was set in a lovely round face. But when her small bow mouth turned up into an enchanting smile, Richard became lost.

"Lord Cranfield," her voice reached into his soul. "It's a pleasure to meet you."

Richard bowed, completely bewildered in the spell she had captured him in with just one glance. At a loss for words, he could only stare at the woman before him, even while he continued to hold her hand in his. What had she done to him?

CHAPTER 6

Patience continued to stare into the face of the handsome man before her. She couldn't do anything less, considering he still held her hand gently in his own. Hazel eyes had always been her downfall, and she swore specks of gold hidden in their depths sparkled like diamonds in the sunshine falling upon them. The lighter highlights in his dark brown hair gave Patience the impression this was a man of leisure who spent a considerable amount of time outside. His classical facial features reminded her of a marbled statue, since he sported that familiar roman nose, chiseled cheeks and a determined square jaw.

"Richard..." Lady Josephine whispered.

Patience cast a glance at Barbara, who only shrugged her shoulders. No help was forthcoming from her step-daughter. She turned her attention back to the man who continued to keep a grasp on her hand. She estimated his age to be perhaps thirty, give or take a couple of years. Older than his sister, she assumed, and most certainly older than herself.

A moment of despair overwhelmed Patience at the sight of Lady Josephine. Would her own stepdaughter Josefina be confused with Lord Cranfield's sister since their names were so similar? Hopefully, this wouldn't become an issue, since they were so different in physical appearance. Inwardly she sighed in the knowledge that this changed nothing. Her priority was Josefina and not the lovely blonde before her.

"Richard," Lady Josephine said more forcibly, and her words at last broke the connection that had seemingly held them spellbound.

Lord Cranfield blinked before he raised her fingertips to kiss the air between his mouth and her gloved hand. "The pleasure is mine, Lady Seahaven," he replied, before he reluctantly let go of her hand.

Conversations continued between Barbara and Lady Josephine, but as far as Patience was concerned, she only had eyes for Lord Cranfield. A viscount, if she remembered her peerage correctly, and the heir to an earl. She finally remembered herself only when Merrilyn and Emma came racing out of the town house.

"Mama," Emma called out, a cross expression on her young face. "Why can't Merry and I have a room to ourselves? We're tired of sharing a nursery with Jane."

Merrilyn stomped her foot. "We're too old to be looked after by Hannah!"

Patience reluctantly turned away from Lord Cranfield, and once more the responsibilities of her position and the family she must see to took precedence over the brief moment of desire that had taken over her entire body. She stole another glance at the viscount, and heat flushed her face. The day had suddenly become overly warm. Another wail from one of her stepdaughters brought her back to the present.

"Girls, you forget yourselves," Patience softly scolded them. "Please return inside where we shall discuss this further. Conversations like this are not meant for the street."

"But, Mama..." Emma whined.

Barbara took a firm hand on the girls. "Inside... both of you. Please excuse me, Lord Cranfield... Lady Josephine," she said but waited at the door for Patience.

"My apologies for my girls. They are just excited to be staying at my cousin's," Patience explained, with a small smile.

Lady Josephine took hold of her brother's arm. "I fondly remember trips to town when I was their age. There is no need to apologize, is there, Richard?" she replied, with a kind smile.

Lord Cranfield appeared as though he were once more lost in his own thoughts before finally replying. "No apologies necessary, my lady. We shouldn't keep you any longer, as I'm certain you wish to get settled."

His sister continued to chatter on. "With the season just beginning, I know we shall cross paths again, Lady Seahaven," she said happily.

Patience nodded her head. "I will look forward to our next meeting."

Lord Cranfield bowed, and Patience turned toward the front of the brick town house while Barbara entered with Jane. Patience hesitated at the door to cast one last look upon Lord Cranfield, who had just assisted his sister into their waiting carriage. He took his place next to her, but once he was settled, his eyes automatically sought out Patience. He tipped his hat to her as they drove by, and Patience watched until their carriage was lost from view.

Shaking her head at where her thoughts had momentarily gone, she entered the town house and breathed in a sigh of relief at the lovely entryway. It had been many years since Patience had visited her cousin. If the rest of Rose's home was as Patience remembered, she was going to be spoiled, and disappointed when they must return to the cottage in Starbrook.

Taking off her bonnet and gloves, she made her way to the master bedroom. The walls were painted a light baby blue while a four-poster bed dominated the room. Being head of the household would allow her the luxury of not having to share a bedroom.

A ruckus from the younger girls bellowing in a very unladylike manner from one of the upper floors caused Patience to roll her eyes. And so it began. Time to get an idea of where everyone would sleep and also where everything was located in the household.

Patience left her room and Josefina was just coming down the stairs. "You best hurry, Patience. Merry and Emma are about to have a go at it again, and they may just try to pull Hannah's hair out."

"I'm coming," Patience replied as Josefina walked up the stairs with her.

"Did you know we had a butler?" she asked quietly.

Her brow rose at her stepdaughter's words. "Rose never mentioned she was keeping any of the staff on," Patience answered, in confusion. *Good heavens, how will we pay him?* They hadn't planned or budgeted for additional staff!

"Well, he's here and down in the kitchen I think. His name is Mal... something. He's very handsome."

"Don't even consider it, Josefina. We're not doing all this so you can make a mesalliance with the household staff," Patience warned, pointing her finger accusingly at her daughter.

"I just said he was handsome. I didn't say I wanted to marry him," she scoffed before running ahead of Patience to find her own room.

Patience was going to have to dig down deep in order to calm her frayed nerves. First, a handsome viscount who couldn't take his eyes from her, reminding her how young she truly was. Second and more importantly, squabbling children who were going to try her patience. She almost laughed, thinking that her name befitted her station in life. Dropping her skirts as she reached the floor with the loudest noise, she lifted her chin to begin their life in York. May it be all she hoped for and more.

CHAPTER 7

Palm Sunday
March 30th, 1817

Richard sat in a pew in York Minster, waiting for Morning Service to begin. They were neither late nor too early, since other parishioners continued to fill the church. Milton, who had arrived yesterday, sat to his left, while Josephine was to his right. They were also accompanied by a distant cousin on his father's side, Mrs. Juliet Elford, who was acting as chaperone for Josephine. She was a kind woman and so completely different than his father that Richard regretted not spending more time with her over the years.

A murmur of voices began to grow in volume from the back of the chapel, and Richard was one of several people who turned in curiosity in order to witness what was causing such a ruckus. And then he saw *her* again, and his heart flipped inside his chest as she came closer. He briefly closed his eyes, wondering if he was imaging this strange fascination with a lady he had only just met. But when he opened his eyes again, he had his answer. His heart stumbled before finding its rhythm again, with a thunderous hard beat loud enough for all the world to hear. She came ever closer, leading the way down the main aisle towards one of several front pews that had apparently been reserved for her and her family... the Dowager Countess of Seahaven.

She was the focus of the entire congregation and, as she strode past his pew, he witnessed her commanding presence despite her short frame. She was a countess, and he shouldn't be surprised she bore the title well. *My, what a beauty!* Yet he felt she was far out of his league. Richard wondered what the devil he was thinking to become mesmerized by a pair of striking blue-grey eyes.

The woman of his recent musings continued forward, holding onto her toddler with curly auburn hair while she nodded her head to several acquaintances. But what surprised Richard the most was the long line of taller young women who followed behind her. *Good heavens!* Was she guardian to all these ladies?

Josephine leaned over to whisper in his ear confirming his fears. "I learned Lady Seahaven was the earl's fifth wife. Those are all her stepdaughters from his previous marriages, the youngest being her own, or so I was told. Can you imagine it, Richard? I highly doubt she would ever wish to remarry. I mean…What man in his right mind would consider her as a potential wife when he would have to deal with an extremely large ready-made family?"

Richard's eyes narrowed when he turned to his sister. "Hush, Josephine, and do not gossip. You know how I loathe it."

She shrugged. "I'm only telling you what I've learned, since you appeared utterly stunned by her the other day. Honestly, you acted as though you were completely smitten, Richard," she teased with a knowing wink.

He gave her another warning look before she gave a short chuckle, snapped her mouth shut, and returned to her quiet conversation with Mrs. Elford.

Milton nudged him while attempting to keep the sly grin from his face. "Interesting to hear you've taken a fancy to a countess. Does she return your affection?"

"Shut up, Milton," Richard ordered only to hear his friend's quiet teasing.

Lady Seahaven began to settle her brood into the two pews while an older lady made her excuses to the women already seated. Josephine leaned over to whisper the woman was Lady Twisden, an aunt to Lady Seahaven and presumably her mother's sister. She made her way to sit next to the countess, who smiled in greeting. The two gave one another a brief hug, as much as the toddler would permit, as the little girl suddenly found the feather in the woman's bonnet an object for her little fingers to grab. Lady Twisden laughed before she cooed over the toddler, giving her chubby cheek a kiss.

Richard watched the countess as though he couldn't take his eyes off her. Josephine's comment had actually hit far too close to its mark, for Patience had been on his mind for the past two days. She turned in the pew, and their eyes met as if she had heard his thoughts. Their gazes held for more than a heartbeat or two, and Richard felt like there was no one else in the huge cathedral. Her smile was ever so slight, when she gave him a tiny nod of her head before she handed the toddler over the seat to what Richard assumed was the girl's nursemaid. With one more glance in his direction, she faced forward, disconnecting their shared moment, leaving Richard feeling the loss.

The service began and ended sooner than Richard realized since he had become completely lost in thought. Obviously he had gone through the motions of responding when needing to purely out of habit. The church began to empty, and Richard watched as the countess and her daughters left their pews. He was about to offer his arm to Josephine when Milton stepped forward.

"Allow me, Lady Josephine... with your permission, of course, Richard," Milton said while Josephine quickly took his arm.

"You're practically family, Milton. Of course, my

brother won't object," Josephine said tossing a glance over her shoulder to Richard.

Mrs. Elford wagged a finger at her charge. "Be sure to stay where I can see you," she ordered, as the couple began to stride toward the entrance of the church. She obviously took her role as chaperon seriously. "Should I be worried?"

"He is a good friend, but that doesn't mean we allow Josephine any more freedom than what would normally be granted her," Richard replied while offering her his arm.

He watched Milton and his sister together. The two were speaking in hushed tones, and he wondered for the first time if perhaps his friend wanted more from Josephine than just being Richard's sister. Did he perhaps wish to court her? Or maybe he only considered her to be like his own sister? His friend was a good man, but perhaps too much like himself in that he knew Milton kept a mistress. That, of course, would never do in Richard's mind, and he would need to find time to speak about Milton's intentions.

Leaving the church, parishioners were gathering in various groups on the front lawn and, as Mrs. Elford went to stand near her charge who was speaking with several of Josephine's acquaintances, Richard took advantage of a rare opportunity that presented itself. The countess was standing alone under a tall oak tree.

He casually strode in her direction, even though the

urge to run before someone in her family demanded her attention overwhelmed him. Instead, he took a deep breath and kept his stride steady. When he bowed before her, she offered her gloved hand, her fingertips gently sliding into his palm. Leaning down, he once more kissed the air between his mouth and her knuckles, all the while wondering how her skin would feel beneath his lips.

"Good morning, Lady Seahaven. It's a delight to see you again," Richard murmured, before he reluctantly released her hand.

"It's a beautiful day, isn't it, Lord Cranfield?" she asked in a breathy whisper.

He tried not to roll his eyes as their conversation was apparently going to be about the weather. Instead, his lips curved upward, and he swore he heard her breath hitch. "The day is as lovely as you are, my lady," he replied and watched the blush rise upon her face at his compliment.

"You are too kind, my lord," she said even as she peered around him, causing Richard to also look to see what drew her attention. "My apologies for becoming distracted with the antics of one of my younger daughter's. It's a bit trying to find a moment of privacy when you have a household of girls under your care. Sometimes they are a bit overwhelming."

Her confession startled him that she would reveal something so personal. Although he wished to stay with her, she obviously wanted to be alone. He hid his disappointment and instead tipped his hat. "Please forgive me for disturbing your solitude," Richard said bowing again before turning to leave.

She surprised him when she reached over and lightly placed her hand upon his arm. "Wait... don't go," she said before her eyes widened, "I mean... please stay if you would like to keep me company."

"You're certain? I do not wish to intrude," Richard said, all the while gazing into her incredible eyes.

Her hand trembled on his arm until she suddenly realized she still held onto him. She gazed down in apparent embarrassment before snatching her hand away. "Yes," she finally murmured before raising her eyes again to stare at him. "Please stay."

"I would be delighted," he replied with a grin. "What brings you to York? I know you are staying at Lady St. Aubyn's town house for she is well acquainted with my family."

"Rose is my cousin on my mother's side and graciously allowed myself and my girls to stay at her home while she is travelling abroad. We are hoping to give my younger stepdaughters a Season here."

"And I am here for the same reason, but for my sister."

She nodded her head. "I am certain Lady Josephine will have no issue finding enough eligible gentlemen to call upon her."

"Yes, it's my fondest hope," Richard agreed before

continuing. "I would think, however, you would prefer to be taking London by storm."

She appeared uncomfortable for a moment before she regained her composure. "We preferred a smaller town. We also wish to attend the races planned in May before we return to Starbrook."

At least now he knew where she resided. "Such a loss for London but a gain for all the gentlemen residing here. Your daughters are lovely... as is their mother," he said while another smile turned up at the corners of his mouth.

"You will turn my head with such compliments, Lord Cranfield." She blushed again, and Richard felt a sudden urge to kiss those perfect lips. Hardly the place or the time but still... how far down her exquisite neck did that blush truly go?

"A compliment that is well deserved, Lady Seahaven," he said while he watched her carefully.

"Patience," she whispered. "My name is Patience... at least when we converse alone, if you don't mind."

His eyes widened at such a bold request. He was about to respond when she gave a light laugh.

"I suppose being a countess does have its advantages, within reason, and as long as I am discreet of course." Her eyes twinkled in merriment while she waited for his answer.

"Then by all means, please call me Richard... when we are alone, that is."

"Richard." His name rolling off her lips sounded like heaven was shining down upon him.

"Patience... You do me a great honor," he replied and watched her whole face light up in delight.

A childish shriek filled the air, and Patience gave a heavy sigh when she realized it came from one of her girls.

"Duty calls, I'm afraid. I have enjoyed our stolen moment together, Richard. I won't soon forget our time here beneath this tree." She reached out her hand as though she were about to place it on his arm before she remembered herself. Clearly she would linger with him in the shade if she could.

"Nor will I, Patience," he murmured while taking in her features as if to memorize each one.

She tipped her head forward in a short nod. "Perhaps the next time we meet, my daughters will remember their manners and not put on such a public display disturbing an otherwise pleasant conversation. As usual, the responsibilities of my life take precedence over dallying the day away at my leisure."

He did his best to hide a smirk, as he could see for himself the younger girls were more than a handful. "I can only hope we can continue our conversation again at another time," he said taking her hand in his. He rubbed the back before raising it to his lips. She gasped when his mouth touched the fabric of her glove before her eyes then twinkled in delight... or was that desire?

Richard hoped for the latter when he tucked her hand in the crook of his arm and escorted her to her family.

She gently held onto his arm, and shivers of desire traveled along his skin. Her nearness made him realize how right it felt to have her this close to his body. She was a countess to remember, and Richard could barely wait until their paths crossed again.

CHAPTER 8

York Assembly Rooms

Patience was as excited as her daughters to be attending their first subscription ball. Barbara was also here chaperoning and had told Patience to enjoy herself. She had given her daughter a look of sheer gratitude. She wasn't sure she remembered how to just be young and carefree.

A miracle had been performed in order to get all the dresses and trim ready for the girls. Walking gowns, ball gowns, and accessories to match! Everyone had pitched in to help and now, studying Josefina, Ivy and Iris, Patience just knew they would find their match in York. They looked lovely, and their dresses could easily be changed so no one would be the wiser that the gown had been worn by one of the other sisters at a different function.

Patience continued to make her way through one room after another while she reminisced about the past several days. Patience knew none of this would have been possible without the thoughtfulness of her cousin Rose when she left letters of introductions for their arrival at her town house. And her girls... every one of them pitched in to ensure they were ready to take York by storm. In the few days they had been here, the women had taken turns in order to not overwhelm any one particular hostess. After all... the Bigglesworth women were a large group to have all in one room.

A ball! It was hard not to appear overly ecstatic about being here. Patience couldn't remember the last time she had attended a ball, but it was certainly before she became pregnant with Jane. Henry hadn't been much of a dancer and also wasn't one to spend his money on fripperies for his young wife. Considering they hadn't been married all that long, she wasn't given enough time to become acquainted with most of the *ton*.

She was perfectly well aware that she wasn't right out of the school room, but she was certainly still young enough at twenty-two to be able to have a bit of fun... within reason of course. She continued to remind herself why she was here. Her daughters came first, and Patience wasn't looking for a husband to call her own.

A pair of mesmerizing hazel eyes flashed inside her head causing her to look around the ballroom to see if Richard was in attendance. *Richard...* she had no idea she could be so bold bas to ask him to call her by her given name, but there was just something about the viscount that drew her to him. She had never been one to believe in love at first sight. She had to be practical, didn't she? But when he took her hand that very first day upon their arrival in York, Patience had to admit, if only to herself, she had been stunned by their connection. She never felt with Henry the way that Richard made her feel. She could drown in his eyes and be perfectly happy to do so for the rest of her life.

Good heavens! Where had such a thought come from? And yet she continued to search through the faces in the crowd in every corner of each room she passed for the man who had charmed her with a gentle smile. Her heart ticked like an over wound clock when she caught a glimpse of him near the balcony doors. Broad shoulders fit perfectly in his dark jacket; his ivory waistcoat was in complete contrast to the rest of his attire that included black trousers encasing his long muscular legs. His cravat was tied in a sophisticated knot that must have had his valet fussing over it for hours. A lock of his dark brown hair fell over his forehead and Patience wanted to push those tresses back into place. He was the stuff dreams were made of and she inwardly gave a heavy sigh at the sight of such a dashing man.

Their eyes met across the room, and he gave her the briefest of nods before walking through the open doorway and out onto a terrace. It was a silent invitation and one she wanted to accept. Patience knew she shouldn't follow him, but all common sense seemed to leave where Richard was concerned. Besides, no harm could be done to meet him outside for only a few moments. Who would miss her?

Trying to keep her pace casual was harder than she thought. She skirted the outside of the dance floor making her way through the crush of people who watched on the sidelines or carried on their own conversations. She saw her girls being watched over by Barbara and she was again grateful that they were being looked after. With no further thoughts except her own personal agenda, she strode through the balcony doors and peered into the shadows to see Richard waiting for her. He held out his hand for her to take and she had a moment of hesitation, as prudence seemed the better course of action.

"Do you trust me?" His hushed baritone voice caused her to shiver in the moonlight and this had nothing to do with being cold.

"Richard... I—"

"Patience... I am asking for you to trust me," he calmly said. "Do you?"

"Yes," she answered him and she could barely make out his smile.

"Then come with me," he said before whisking her away into the night.

He seemed to know where he was going as he went down several steps and onto a garden path. She gazed back over her shoulder wondering where he was taking her.

"My girls—" she began before he interrupted her.

"We won't be gone long or go that far."

"Promise?" she whispered into the night.

"Yes. I promise. You are perfectly safe with me, my dear," he exclaimed and, true to his word, he halted near a gazebo awash in the moonlit sky. A romantic setting that caused Patience's heart to race.

"This is a lovely place, Richard, but—"

He turned her into his arms, and Patience couldn't object, not when she had been envisioning this in her dreams for the past several days. "I know this is sudden, Patience, but I've been dying to do this ever since we met," he said brushing a lock of her hair behind her ear before cupping her cheek.

She leaned into the palm of his hand. "What have you been wanting to do?" she asked hoping he wouldn't find her undesirable but also praying he would kiss her no matter that they had just met.

"This..."

She held her breath while his mouth slowly descended upon her own. At first, gentle, exploring to see just how much she might allow. A nip at her lower lip to tease her caused her gasp of surprise giving him the opening he had apparently been waiting for. His tongue dipped in to take hungry possession of her mouth, and she was more than willing to learn this new dance together.

She wasn't new to the intimacies between a couple but Richard's kiss flared into a burning flame in the pit of her stomach. Henry had never bothered with such affections, and yet, with Richard, she wanted to explore every aspect of what he could bring her. Did this make her one of those wanton women?

He deepened their kiss, and Patience wound her arms around his neck to play with the edges of his hair at his collar. His groan would have caused her to smile if she had been able to perform such a task. He brought her tight against his chest, and she could not mistake his arousal. She should have been shocked but this only made her want more of this man than he could obviously give her standing in a garden.

Whether he could read her thoughts or he just realized how entirely inappropriate their situation could become if they were found, he ended their kiss, leaving her wanting to return to his arms. He placed both hands on her cheeks, running his thumbs over them before giving her another quick kiss.

"Better than I could have ever imagined," he murmured before he bent down to place his forehead to her own.

"Was it?" she asked shaking from the experience of what almost felt like her first real kiss.

He jerked back before peering down upon her with a frown. "You didn't enjoy it?"

Her eyes widened at the thought. "Oh yes, Richard. It was wonderful!"

"I had hoped you felt something between us and I wasn't imagining our connection," he said before he scanned her features.

"I would be lying if I told you I didn't know what you were talking about, for I have felt it too," she admitted with a smile. "But, as lovely as this little interlude has been, I must return inside. I cannot risk being ostracized by Society, which would ruin the Season for my daughters."

"I understand, but I needed to have just a moment with you," he stated before holding out his arm. They began to walk side by side towards the building. "Will you save me a dance, Patience?"

"If I could, I would dance only with you for the entire evening," she replied giving his arm a gentle squeeze.

"I would be truly honored and cannot wait until we meet again. Will you be attending the al fresco party at Tyrell House?"

"Yes, the entire family plans to attend. If you are also attending, this will give me something extra special to look forward to."

"The night is still young, but I understand I will not be able to monopolize all your time. I, too, must see to my responsibilities with my sister, even though our cousin is chaperoning." He halted before leading her back up the stairs and gave her another kiss. It was far shorter than earlier, but she was happy to receive it all the same.

"I'll see you inside then," she said, reluctant to leave his side.

"And don't forget to save me a dance," he urged before raising her hand to his lips.

"I won't," she replied giving him a bright smile.

"I'll let you go in first so as not to cause suspicion."

She turned one last time to look at the man who had somehow stolen her heart. Who would have thought she would possibly find love in York? Miracles did happen.

CHAPTER 9

Richard casually strode along the somewhat manicured lawn at the al fresco party. The owners of Tyrell House were in the process of bringing the estate back to life after years of apparent neglect. Those in attendance didn't seem to mind. But what really held Richard's interest was his conversation with the new Viscount Tyrell, John Bentley, and his cousin, Captain James Bentley, who were the driving force behind a proposed equestrian park. The two men had put on the entertainment today to gain interest in their horse training facility, along with a newly constructed practice race course. Richard was more than interested and looked forward to learning more at a future date.

Josephine was sitting with a group of friends on a blanket having luncheon, and he felt she was in good hands with Mrs. Elford sitting at a nearby table. Instead of intruding on gossiping women, he took the opportunity to wander among groups of various people, stopping on occasion to say hello to friends but, more importantly, looking for Patience and her family.

Richard tipped his hat to Lady Harriet Staunton to whom he had been introduced earlier in the day. She gave a brief nod and continued her way across the lawn with another acquaintance. Josephine had whispered that Lady Harriet was yet another cousin to Patience, although he couldn't dismiss the uncanny resemblance to the other Bigglesworth sisters.

He continued forward in his quest to find one particular lady in a sea of women. Childish laughter finally caught his attention, drawing his gaze to a nearby lake. And there she was, giggling at the antics of her younger daughters who danced around the blanket she was sitting on with her toddler. What was odd, however, was seeing Milton chuckling along with them, including a few of the daughters Richard had yet to be introduced to. He lessened the distance to reach Patience, wondering if he had been wrong that Milton held some affection for his sister and instead was interested in the countess herself or one of her eligible daughters.

Milton had his back to him as Richard approached but what came next made him stop.

"I would not lie to you, Lady Seahaven," Milton confessed holding up his hands. "Richard and I were always trying to outdo one another when we were lads. One day when we were perhaps thirteen years of age, he swore he could swim to the other side of my father's lake faster than I. I tried to warn him that this particular section of the lake was shallower than the rest. With a dare for me to join him, he jumped in and slipped on the mud beneath his feet causing him to go under. He came up for air covered in mud, silt, tangled in the roots of water lilies, and dragging some of the flowers with him when he came out to the bank. To see a couple of lilies dangling from the top of his head as he emerged is a sight I have never forgotten."

Young Emma laughed, clapping her hands in delight. "He must have appeared like a rising sea monster only prettier with all those flowers!"

Richard groaned before placing a hand on Milton's shoulder. "You couldn't tell them something more flattering than that fiasco?" he inquired with a smirk.

"Can you blame me? It's one of our greatest memories from our youth," Milton exclaimed before leaning in to quietly whisper in his ear. "Besides... it was a tale more inclined for the amusement of ladies than some of our more daring escapades."

Richard cleared his throat hoping his friend's words hadn't been overheard. "And what brought this particular conversation on?" Richard asked good naturedly.

"It's my fault," Emma chimed in. "I wanted to go near the lake but Mama said I might slip on the bank and ruin my dress. Lord Sutton said he'd share a funny story with us."

"I'd rather play in the lake. We never get to have any fun," Merrilynn chimed in.

Emma twirled around in a circle. "Not true, sister. We're here today, and I'm going to enjoy every minute of the party before Mama says we have to go home!"

Patience smiled at the girls while her toddler came and plopped herself on her lap. She gave brief introductions to the stepdaughters Richard had yet to meet before she continued. "As you can see, we can be a somewhat rambunctious group, and it was too nice a day to leave the younger children at home."

Richard nodded. "No reason why they shouldn't enjoy the outing. With the weather particularly warm for April, an al fresco party is just the thing." Were they chatting about the weather again, and this time initiated by him? He almost groaned aloud. Surely, he could think of another topic of witty conversation to amuse her besides the weather.

Milton excused himself to speak to the other young ladies on the next blanket giving Richard a small amount of privacy to have Patience all to himself.

"You look lovely today, Lady Seahaven."

"Thank you, Lord Cranfield," she said bouncing the child on her lap.

Complimenting her came as easily as taking his next breath, and her blush only enhanced her beauty. Dressed in a white gown, the square cut of her garment just rising above her breasts was decorated in tiny embroidered rosebuds, and he wondered if she had taken the time to sew them herself. Not that it mattered if she could sew or not... He was generally more interested in getting a woman out of her gown than into it. But the dress became her along with her matching bonnet. Was he becoming some sort of dandy? Thinking of the intricate detail of a gown would be more in line with something his friend George would consider and talk about. God forbid if Richard was becoming more like him!

As he continued to watch Patience with her daughter, Richard had a vision of his own child held in the arms of the countess. Given their kiss the other night, he knew his feelings were reciprocated no matter that they had only just met. Could this possibly be the start of something that could last a lifetime? Only time would tell. If anything, they had a friendship that was blooming right before his very eyes, and he had to admit he had missed her company since the ball. A smile came to his face as he remembered having the opportunity to have two dances with her. A waltz had kept her in his arms. A faster-paced dance kept their fingertips touching and laughter on their lips. At the time, he had wished he could have danced the night away with her. However, that would have caused a scandal.

He realized Patience was struggling to rise with a wiggly toddler balanced on her hip. Rushing over, Richard held onto her elbow until she finally stood on solid ground. She raised those glorious blue-grey eyes to him in obvious gratitude.

"My chivalrous knight coming to my rescue," she quietly said, beaming up at him with those glorious eyes before continuing, "Will you perhaps show up next on a white steed?" Her twinkling eyes told him much, and he couldn't resist the smile that turned up the corners of his mouth.

"If my lady so commands me, I will be more than happy to come to your rescue whenever you have need of me. I just so happen to have a white horse in my stables to await your pleasure."

Her laughter rang out, causing Richard's heart to swell. "I really think I'm going to have to be careful around you, my lord. You continue to turn my head with such flattery," she teased.

He leaned forward. "I would never tire of giving you the compliments you so deserve, my dearest lady," he murmured for her ears alone, before stepping back as protocol dictated.

Before she could comment, the squirming toddler made it known she no longer wished to be held by her mother. Patience put her down and before she could grab hold of her hands, the young girl wobbled over to Richard and grabbed him around his legs. His eyes widened in surprise until the little crumb crawler with curly auburn hair raised her blue eyes up to him and spoke.

"Papa up!" she demanded holding up her tiny hands for him to take.

"Jane!" Patience moaned in embarrassment, before some of her daughters all began speaking at once.

"Did she—"

"She did and—"

"Good heav—"

"We'll never live this down!"

Milton was doing everything in his power not to burst out in amusement while Richard could only stare at the little urchin who smacked his legs and repeated her demand only louder.

"Papa up!"

With one look at the horrified expression from her mother, Richard reached down to grab Jane who finally settled down once her demands had been met. Chubby hands patted him on his cheeks before a childish giggle escaped her.

"Hello, little moppet," Richard cooed to the girl, who stuck her thumb in her mouth and rested her head on his shoulder. It only took a few minutes with the Bigglesworth women whispering among themselves to realize Jane had fallen asleep in his arms.

"Lord Cranfield, I must apologize for—" Patience began but Richard quietly interrupted her.

"There is no need, Lady Seahaven. I am more than happy to become Jane's pillow for her nap."

"Perhaps, if you would be so kind, you could carry Jane to our carriage." If he had thought Patience's blush could become any deeper from his past experiences with her, then Richard was wrong. She snatched a fan attached to her wrist and began waving it before her face as though it was on fire.

"I'd be more than happy to carry her for you, my lady," Richard replied, trying to catch the woman's eyes. But she had other ideas and looked everywhere but in his direction.

Patience started to gather her belongings left on the blanket before instructing her younger daughters. "Come along, girls. You can return home with Jane and your nursemaid."

"We don't want to leave with Hannah," the girls complained in unison.

But a softly spoken warning from their mother quieted the pair down. "Do not wake your sister, girls. Now go with Hannah to our carriage."

The girls pouted, knowing their time at the party was over, and Richard did all in his power not to smirk at their attempts to change their mother's mind.

While the girls ran ahead, Richard reached over to offer his arm to Patience. Her hand trembled once she placed it into the crook of his arm. "There is no need to be embarrassed, my lady. Jane is young and the mistake is an honest one," he said quietly, although she continued to refuse to meet his eyes.

"I will never be able to face you again," she moaned causing Richard to stop his progress to her carriage.

He quickly looked to ensure they were for the most

part alone. Since no one was within hearing distance, he felt no need for formalities. "Please don't say that, Patience. I would like us to continue to see one another to see if we might suit."

"I'm not sure this is a good idea, Richard," she said so calmly that he was afraid that what had started between them had already ended. "You make me forget my true purpose of being here in York. My daughters must come first before my own needs."

"Of course, you must think of your daughters, but that doesn't mean we cannot continue as before. Don't let the words of your youngest be the reason why you do not wish to see me."

"I-I need time," she choked out, and he could see she was trying not to cry.

"Then take all the time you need," Richard replied knowing he couldn't say anything more to change her mind... at least not now when her embarrassment over her daughter calling him papa was so fresh in her mind.

They reached her carriage and she turned to him. "Good day, Lord Cranfield."

"Good day, Lady Seahaven," he replied as he realized she was going to join her daughters and leave the party.

As he handed the small child into the arms of the nursemaid, he wondered if perhaps his heart was being won over not only by the countess herself but her bevy of daughters as well.

CHAPTER 10

She was a coward. There were no other words for her to describe the past week of refusing Richard's notes so she might receive him. The bouquet of roses sitting in a crystal vase in the upper parlor taunted her as if questioning her sanity for not speaking to the man. He had done everything right in his attempts to put her at ease. But how could she ever forget the brief look that flashed in those hazel eyes when Jane had called him papa? She bit her lower lip as the memory rolled over and over again in her mind. Oh, the horror! She couldn't be with a man who didn't love her daughters.

He made up for it, of course. Watching him hold Jane protectively in his arms was one of the most beautiful things Patience had ever witnessed. Jane obviously felt comfortable enough to fall asleep on his shoulder, and who could blame her. Patience wouldn't mind being held in those magnificent strong arms again, and she had dreamed of him every night since the *incident*. She barely knew the man, and yet there was no way for her to get over the fact that, by having these unexpected feelings for Richard, she was not concentrating enough on the issue at hand. Seeing her daughters engaged to men worthy of them.

She turned her back on the blooms to gaze out the window facing the street while she tried not to chew at her fingernail. The object of her recent frustrations came out of his town house with his sister as they walked past her own house. She drew back from the window when he looked up as if to catch a glimpse of her. Was that disappointment that appeared to be briefly etched upon his brow? How handsome he appeared while he escorted Lady Josephine on their walk.

Patience knew she was being foolish, or was she? Stepping forward again, she moved back the sheer drapery in order to continue watching him until he was out of sight. Her mind wandered over the whisperings overheard during several events in York. They said he had the reputation of a renowned rake in London and currently kept a mistress. Patience was never one to base her judgement for a person because of gossip, but perhaps this was another reason why she hesitated on furthering her association with the man. Was he perhaps a bachelor only looking to take advantage of a widow? She wasn't sure her heart could take being hurt or easily dismissed if Richard's only thought was a brief carnal liaison.

She gave a heavy sigh. Nothing Richard had done had suggested the rumors were true and obviously she had let stupid tittle tattle rule her thinking where the viscount was concerned. He had been nothing but a gentleman while in her presence, and she should listen to her heart. Any concerns she may have briefly had about Richard's sincerity were unfounded, or so she hoped. Patience turned away from the image of Richard and from thoughts of their moonlit kiss.

Her eyes once more traveled to the roses that mocked her in her indecisiveness regarding the handsome gentleman. Could she honestly put aside the man for whom her heart called? Her mental struggle conflicted with her duties as head of the household. But it seemed a shame to give up on a chance at love while her own daughters searched for it themselves.

"Patience?"

Her name was called from across the room. She had been too lost in thought to keep up with the conversation going on around her. If she had bitten any harder on her lip, she would have drawn blood.

"I'm coming," she replied, as she made her way across the room to sit at the table with Doro and Chloe, who was the daughter of Henry's fourth wife by a previous marriage and so Doro's stepsister. This was the reality of her life—all three of them were twenty-two years of age, but Patience was head of this household. The two had their heads together looking at the figures Doro kept in neat columns.

"We can manage it, Patience," Doro exclaimed. "With the help of your aunt, Lady Twisden, and Chloe's brother Martin, Lord Tavistock, we'll have enough to purchase an entire garden of flowers and to pay the servers and musicians on the twenty-second of April."

Chloe smiled and reached over to take Patience's hand giving it a squeeze. "My brother was only too happy to contribute, especially since you graciously offered to allow me to be a co-hostess."

"We could never afford the hall without your brother's help along with your connections, Doro," Patience said, nodding while Mrs. Crewe carried in a tray holding a teapot and cups. Hannah followed behind with a plate of little cakes. Patience began to pour once the tray was set before her.

She took a sip of her tea, hoping the brew would calm her. "What about decorations?" she asked reaching for a sweet Doro had baked this morning. "I know between us, the kitchen will be taken care of. If you have these delightful desserts, we'll have all of Society calling at our door to find out who is baking for us."

Doro smiled. "We can have Iris and Ivy head into town to pick up what we'll need, and I'm certain they'll be more than happy to create anything to make the place our own. We'll have the day prior to the date of the ball to decorate plus the day afterwards to clean everything up."

Chloe nodded. "I'm sure we can make adjustments as needed if we forget anything."

Patience nodded. "I know I've said this more times than I can count, but honestly I could never have accomplished all this without everyone's help. You don't know how much it means to me that everyone has joined together to give Josefina, Iris, and Ivy a Season."

"They're our best chance of making a match," Doro answered finishing her tea. "I'd best go take stock of the kitchen to see what other supplies we may need."

"I'll come with you. You can put me to work making lists." Chloe rose. She placed a hand on Patience's shoulder. "Everything will work out just fine so there's no need to worry."

"Was I worrying?" Patience asked, gazing up at the young woman before her.

Chloe gave a light giggle. "Well, the frown upon your brow tells me you're worrying about something. Honestly, Patience, everything that is meant to be will be..."

Patience smiled in response as she watched the two women leave. Of course she was worrying, but it had nothing to do with the ball and everything to do with a man whose hazel eyes haunted her every waking moment. There was something about Richard she couldn't easily dismiss, and in that exact moment she realized she didn't want to. For the first time in her entire adult life, Patience was going to think of herself and what may be with a man who made her heart sing.

Her decision made, she left the parlor to go downstairs to her bedroom. A desk sat against one of the walls and she pulled out the chair to take out paper in order to pen her note.

Forgive my foolishness.

Would you like to meet somewhere to talk?

Affectionately, P

Sealing the note with wax, Patience sent for Hannah to deliver her missive to Richard, knowing he currently wasn't at home. Hannah, bless her soul, didn't even blink but gave her a smile that looked as though she was on a mission of grave importance. Patience supposed she was, in many ways. It was a bold move on her part... asking a gentleman to meet with her, possibly alone. But there was no going back now, and all she had to do was wait for a reply upon his return home. She had the notion the waiting was going to drive her insane.

Keeping busy would restrain her from watching the clock slowly tick away. She went up to Jane's room. The little girl became excited when Patience entered. Jane was the light of Patience's life, and she picked her daughter up from her crib and tightly hugged the child to her. Placing a blanket on the floor, Patience put some wooden blocks down along with a cloth doll so they could play together.

The morning went by and faded away to early afternoon before Hannah appeared in the doorway, her eyes twinkling mischievously from the prospect of what she held in her hands. Patience was sitting in a rocking chair, Jane sleeping in her lap. Standing up, she gently placed her daughter back in her crib before turning to the nursemaid.

A smile escaped Patience when she took the note from Hannah, along with a bouquet of lilies in a lovely decorated vase. They weren't the water lilies Lord Sutton had spoken of but he had painted such a detailed picture of a young Richard that Patience suddenly relived the memory in her mind. A short snort, accompanied by a light laugh, caused a blush to rush to her face before she returned her attention to what she held in her hands. The colorful flower arrangement was a lovely reminder of an afternoon filled with promises if she had only stayed longer to enjoy his company.

Leaving her daughter's room knowing Hannah would take care of the child when she woke from her nap, Patience returned to her own bedroom to read Richard's reply in privacy. Setting the lilies on the desk so she could enjoy them, she went to sit on her bed, fluffing the pillows behind her before breaking the seal on his letter.

Dinner. My place. Tomorrow night at nine.
Yours, R

. . .

A startled gasp escaped her, but the fluttering in her chest more than spoke her feelings at what this evening might entail. There was only one reply she could give him, and she went to the desk to quickly pen her answer.

Yes!

CHAPTER 11

R ichard gazed around the drawing room wondering what he had forgotten in his attempt to create a romantic setting perfect for his countess. Candles were lit, illuminating the room in a soft glow. A small repast for two awaited only the occupants to seat themselves at the small intimate table. He thought of filling the room with flowers but realized that might be a bit much considering the number of bouquets he had been sending to the lady in the past week. He was certain the person that owned the flower shop had been more than pleased by his constant purchases.

Originally, he had planned for them to be seated in the dining room but the close proximity to the master bedroom would be even too much for him to handle. He had never wanted a woman more than he wanted Patience, but he had no intention of scaring her off. The fact she had accepted his invitation in the first place meant she had put her trust in him. He knew it was fragile, at best. He wouldn't ruin their night together or rush her into anything she wasn't ready for.

Seeing that everything was in place and only needed the lady of his musings to complete the perfect setting, he left the room to head downstairs to the ground floor. He had given the servants the night off. Josephine and their cousin were off to one of the many balls being hosted this evening. This left only Richard and his lady to enjoy the night alone together.

As he descended the last step into the inner hall, the grandfather clock chined nine. As the last bong resounded throughout his town house, the rap of the knocker on the front door could be heard. Opening the door, the light from the entryway shone upon a woman in a long blue cloak. A hood hid her face but Richard would have known this lady no matter what she was wearing. She quickly entered and Richard shut the door before the hood was removed from her head.

Patience... he took his time looking his fill while the lady unfastened the clasp at her throat. His manners kicked in when she handed him her cloak and he took the garment from her and placed it on a nearby table that of late had been filled with invitations. She took off her gloves and placed them on top of her coat before turning to gaze upon him.

He took her hands in his and for the first time felt her soft fingertips glide into his palms. He raised her hands to his lips, kissing each one before he held out his arm.

"Are you hungry?" he asked, watching her as they began to climb the stairs to the next floor.

Her look bore into his when she gazed upon him from the corner of her eyes. "For food?" she teased, causing Richard to almost trip on a step. Her eyes shined brightly while she suppressed a laugh.

"I suppose that's a good place to start," he replied when they reached the landing.

"That was probably a little too forward of me," she said softly with downcast eyes.

"I didn't mind," he replied before lifting her chin, so she had no choice but to look at him.

"Truly?"

"I want you to be yourself around me and feel comfortable enough to speak your mind. I don't mind your playful bantering. I actually find it quite refreshing."

"I would only dare to do so when we are alone."

He brushed back a lock of her hair that had fallen from her coiffure. "Then I am glad I've given the servants the night off."

He ushered her into the drawing room and her gasp of surprise made his heart rejoice, knowing she was pleased with his efforts. He had never been the romantic type, but for Patience he wanted to give her the moon if it would but make her happy.

"Richard! You shouldn't have gone to so much trouble," she whispered before stepping on the tips of her toes to place a gentle kiss on his cheek. The warmth of her breath was almost his undoing as heat radiated throughout his body.

"It was no trouble, my dear," he said holding out a chair for her.

"It's lovely."

He took the silver dome off their plates and their conversation was casual as they ate their meal. They spoke a little of their childhoods and families, of their dreams from their youths, and how their lives were far different than what they expected when they were young. She appeared somewhat reluctant to speak about her relationship with her late husband and Richard didn't push the issue. Nor did she mention her association with the new earl. He wanted the evening to go smoothly and not have any unpleasantries infringe on their time together.

With dinner over, he went to a sideboard and poured her a sherry and a brandy for himself while Patience made her way over to a couch. Arranging the skirt of her dress, she accepted the drink and took a sip. She appeared more relaxed than during dinner, and he was thankful she was letting her guard down around him. He sat down next to her, and he was pleasantly surprised when she took his hand. He raised her fingertips to his mouth giving them a brief kiss.

"You must be wondering about all my stepdaughters," she remarked after putting her glass down on the table in front of them.

"Only if you wish to speak of them. I am assuming your story has an ending that isn't exactly a pleasant one." He rubbed the back of her hand with his thumb and continued to hold her gaze.

She began giving a quick version of her husband's past marriages, ending with her own and her daughter Jane.

"I was apparently his last hope of gaining a son to inherit his title. One would have thought after all the daughters he had sired he would have known this was probably unlikely." Her attempt at a smile seared into his heart, but her tone had an edge to it, as though there was still more to her story. She took up her glass again, and he assumed she needed the liquor to continue her tale.

"Did you love him?" Where the bloody hell did that question come from?

She almost choked on the sherry. He patted her back before she set the glass down and nodded she was fine. "Love never played into my relationship with my husband. He was an end to a means. That must sound as if I was only after his money, which was not the case." She took a deep breath before turning to fully look upon him. "My father was a baker, my mother disowned from her family because they felt she married beneath her. I married Henry because I thought this would help my family. My parents convinced me this would be my way into Society."

"A dutiful daughter," Richard murmured before she continued her story.

"To be fair, Henry was indulgent with his daughters when he noticed them and was particularly fond of Josefina. He died before Jane was born, so he never knew he had sired another daughter. My parents passed away two days later from a carriage accident. In the end, there was little left of what was due me and the girls, or at least that was what I was told. Heaven only knows how Henry squandered the money before he died."

"You have had your share of misfortune for one so young." Richard frowned, wondering how this woman had been surviving. "Surely the new earl provided for you?"

"He gave me but a pittance, including what was left as a dowry for the girls once they wed." She placed her hand to her mouth as if to stop the words. He was about to tell her he didn't need to hear more when her voice burst out in embarrassment. "Good heavens! What you must think of me, baring my soul to you like this."

"I think you are incredible, Patience," he murmured giving hand a squeeze. "Please finish your story but only if you wish to do so."

She quickly composed herself, and with a nod of her head continued. "The new earl then basically threw us out of Seahaven with nothing more than the clothes we could carry. Fortunately, I inherited my parent's cottage in Starbrook after they passed. We've been living there ever since."

It was worse than he had imagined, but this only made him admire the woman before him even more. "I could make some inquires to see if the Earl has robbed you of monies to which you were entitled, or perhaps there was a hidden will. That is, if you wish it." Richard watched Patience who brought her eyes up to meet his own. He expected tears and instead he saw gratitude shining on her face.

"That is kind of you, Richard, but I want nothing from that man or his controlling wife. As far as I'm concerned, they don't exist. I look forward to the day when some situation occurs and they get their comeuppance. I won't have to do a thing to play any role in whatever fiasco comes their way, and I can just sit back and watch it happen."

A chuckle escaped him and her return smile warmed his heart. "You are truly a wonder, my lady. But how have you survived all this time since your husband's death?"

She raised her chin. "We've been capitalizing on whatever traits could earn us money, not that we've let anyone know in Society. All of my older stepdaughters have done their part to help the household. They have even sacrificed their own portion of their dowries to pool the funds together for the younger girls. Hence, our time here in York."

"And what of you? What part have you played other than being the stepmother to all these women?" he asked quietly.

"I've been baking, bread mostly, to sell in the local village," she replied honestly, before taking another sip of her sherry.

He had the vision of this lady rising from her slumber before the day had even begun and he was certain he wasn't wrong in his assumption. "What a brave woman you are, Patience." He ran the back of his fingers down her cheek.

"I've had to become a survivor, Richard. I would do anything for my girls."

"I applaud your devotion to your family, my dear. But still... what of yourself?"

Her brow rose at his question. "Whatever do you mean?"

"What do you desire for yourself, Patience?" He watched her eyes widen at his husky tone.

She watched him intently before a small smile graced her lips. "I suppose I want what every woman wants... to find someone to love. Someone who can help erase past memories that are unpleasant and build a bright future together in a loving household. However, not many men would like to marry a woman who has so many mouths to feed."

"Surely you do not think I am one of those men?"

She tilted her head while she studied him before her

warm smile gave him her answer. "I wouldn't be here, Richard, if I thought you were."

His heart swelled at her words and there was only one thing he could do after she had confessed her deepest thoughts. He kissed her as she was meant to be kissed. Lovingly. Gently. And as she became folded into his arms, he had the notion of never letting her go.

Any thoughts of where the night might proceed left him, but he gave himself into this one moment together as he deepened their kiss. It was a beginning and a promise of what was to come. The start of building on a relationship he knew in his heart could last them a lifetime.

By the time he had thoroughly kissed the woman he was growing to love, the grandfather clock chimed in the downstairs entryway, telling him he needed to let her go home. His sister would be returning soon and he didn't want Patience to be found here alone. Her disappointment when he escorted her down to the floor below was written all over her face. She wanted more... as did he.

But he respected her enough that he would not take her to his bed this night even while a part of him warred with his mind. They would have plenty of time to grow their relationship, and Richard looked forward to the coming days where he could spend more time with his lovely countess.

CHAPTER 12

For days, Patience felt as though she had been walking on air. Her step was lighter and she was happier than she ever remembered. There was only one person who was the cause for her sudden change from her every day normal and boring routine, and that was Richard. He brought her out of the gloom that had become her life and gave her hope for a future together.

But she had no time to contemplate the man who had filled her every waking hour, or dreams for that matter. Not with the ball she was hosting with her aunt, stepdaughters and Chloe about to begin. She was certain they had forgotten something, but for the life of her she couldn't think of any detail that had been left out from their efforts.

Everything appeared in place, and Patience was proud of the work her family had done to decorate Smithson's

Assembly Room. The girls had created lovely favors in the form of tiny birds in a rainbow of colors that graced the round supper tables. The twins' trompe l'oeil on fabric stretched across the back wall, transforming it into a window on an Italianate garden. The ballroom floor gleamed from a recent polish of wax giving off the appearance of a golden glow. Boughs decorated with camellia blossoms had been brought in from the garden and were placed in various places adding to the beauty of the place. The musicians had arrived and were in the upper gallery tuning their instruments. White candles hung from the chandeliers as footmen came to light them. Yes... the place looked marvelous and only awaited their guests to fill the rooms for the evening.

Satisfied that all was ready, Patience went upstairs to a room reserved for her daughters to get dressed. Before she even came to the door, she could hear their laughter. It was an exciting time for all of them, and one they had been waiting on for several months. Patience could only pray that all their efforts would result in possible engagements.

Opening the door, Patience eyes began to water when she saw all her lovely daughters dressed in their finest. Susana had indeed performed a miracle with her sewing talents and no one would have guessed these dresses had previously been worn. Even Bess had taken a break from her translations in order to enjoy the evening. The Bigglesworth women were going to be the center of attention tonight, if the view before her was any indication.

Patience wiped a tear from her eye before she clapped her hands to get everyone's attention. "You all look lovely tonight and I couldn't be prouder of each and every one of you."

"Have the guests begun to arrive?" Barbara asked while putting on her gloves.

"The footmen are lighting the candles as we speak so we should be in our places downstairs when the first carriage arrives. The younger girls can head into the ballroom. Aunt Honoria, Bess, Susana, Lord Tavistock, and I will stand in the receiving line," Patience said, smiling in anticipation for the night to begin. She took another glance at her girls and they were all impeccably attired.

Ivy placed a fan around her wrist that would also act as a dance card. "I'm so excited. Just think, our first ball that we are actually hosting!"

Her twin looped her arm through her sisters as they headed out the door. "I can barely wait for a dance with a certain Captain," Iris was heard to say before disappearing down the hallway.

Patience noticed Josefina's eyes sparkled in delight but it was her smile that made her stepdaughter appear even more lovely than she usually did. She strode over to the girl and took her hand. "Is everything alright, dearest?" she asked wondering what secret the girl held to herself.

Josefina kissed her cheek. "Everything is... perfect."

The rest of the women began to leave the room leaving herself and Chloe alone. Patience went to a full-length mirror and checked her gown. The blue muslin gown brought out the color of her eyes and she pondered if a certain gentleman would agree with her.

Chloe picked up her fan. "Do you think it will work?" she asked waiting for Patience's reply.

With one last glance in the mirror, she took a deep breath before turning around. "Let's find out."

What followed was an interminable amount of time in a receiving line, greeting her guests. Invitations had been sent out to anyone in York of any importance and the faces became a blur as people continued to enter the Assembly Room. That was until *he* entered, and Patience was certain the world had stopped spinning on its axis.

It was hard for her to ignore the man who made her heart hammer in her chest with just one look from those brilliant hazel eyes. He took in her appearance while observing her from afar before the corner of his mouth lifted up into a small roguish grin. He was speaking with Lady Josephine but he continued to sneak peaks at Patience. Richard appeared impatient for his turn to be presented to her, and she shared the sentiment.

Were her emotions just as transparent as the feelings she detected flashing across Richard's face as he drew near? Adoration... happiness... and most of all, did she envision love reflected in his features? Or was it just desire to finish what they had started one night? She could no longer deny Richard awoke a passion in her that had been dormant her entire life. Was it truly possible she was in love with the man, although she had yet to speak the words aloud?

And then he was before her, bowing over her hand, his mouth respectfully hovering over her fingertips when all she wanted to do was throw herself into his arms. A few short pleasantries were murmured before he whisked his sister away, and Patience immediately felt his loss. She was certain she wouldn't recuperate until she was once more in his presence. Yes... this must be what the poets called love. It couldn't be anything less.

As one of the hostesses for the ball, Patience was kept busy for the majority of the evening. The dancing had begun, but she had yet to have the opportunity to enjoy the music. She had finally found a moment to sit down, and she wished she could take off her shoes to give her feet some relief. But all that changed when a certain gentleman made his way across the room in a determined stride.

Richard had sought her out, holding his hand out for her to take. His silent request to dance with her was answered when she lightly placed her fingertips into the palm of his hand. He led her to the ballroom. The music for a waltz began, and Richard put his hand at the back of her waist. She almost sighed aloud when tingling sensations rushed throughout her body. She was never going to make it through the dance let alone what was left of the evening with his continual perusal of her whenever they were in the same room.

"I couldn't wait any longer to have you in my embrace," Richard murmured in that seductive tone that would make any woman swoon. She stumbled at his words because they echoed her own sentiments. He quickly covered for her blunder and pulled her slightly closer into his arms. "Steady, my lady. I have you now."

"If you only knew how much I would like to have a private moment with you." Her hushed reply caused another wicked grin to spread across his mouth making Patience eager for his kiss.

"I feared if I didn't take the opportunity to dance with you now, your ball would be over, and I would lose my chance. Perhaps we can talk in a while when this crush begins to disperse for the evening," he said hopefully before he whirled her around causing her to become light headed.

"I would like that very much." She smiled into those mesmerizing hazel eyes and decided to enjoy this moment together while it lasted.

The dance continued, but Richard's features suddenly changed and not for the better. One moment he appeared completely at ease, and the next Patience swore his complexion paled before a muscle in his jaw started to tick. His eyes narrowed while peering across the room, and Patience attempted to see what had angered him.

"What's wrong, Richard," she asked nervously before he composed himself by looking into her eyes. But something had happened for he didn't appear as carefree as he had but moments before.

"It's nothing." His short sharp retort said otherwise, but she wasn't allowed to comment further. The dance ended. He bowed politely. She curtsied in return and, with another brief bow, he abruptly left her side without another word.

Patience was unsure if she should follow him or not, but she certainly was going to find out what in the world just happened to her perfect evening that suddenly was anything but!

CHAPTER 13

Richard left the dance floor with barely a word to Patience. Nostrils flaring, he clenched his hands into fists at his side when he went from room to room searching for someone who shouldn't be here. How the devil was it possible *she* was here? He knew damn well she hadn't been invited.

A flash of her green muslin gown caught has attention as she rounded the stairs and he followed behind at a slower pace. His attempts to appear casual warred with his urge to rush up the steps to confront her. Peering into one room after another he finally found her as though she had posed specifically to gain his attention near a window, the backlight from the candles casting her in a soft glow. She was the complete opposite of the woman he had just left—darkness to the light that was all Patience. But none of that mattered at the moment. He crossed the space between them and grabbed her arm.

"What the hell are you doing here, Penelope?" he hissed. His cold glare should have been a warning, but her eyes glazed over with need and desire. He had seen that look before. She was in a temper and was out to prove whatever point she planned to make. Another reason he no longer kept her as his mistress.

"Richard, darling... I thought you would be happy to see me," she purred before rubbing her hand along the edges of his jacket. "How handsome you are this evening. I've never seen you look better."

He threw his hands up and backed away from her. Running his fingers along the back of his neck, he made another attempt to figure out what his ex-mistress wanted. "You didn't answer me. Why are you here in York... at this ball?"

She came over to him and, before he could stop her, she brushed her fingertips across his brow. "You really shouldn't frown, darling. You'll get wrinkles before your time."

"I won't ask you again, Penelope." He wanted her out of here before the situation got out of hand.

She went back toward the window to move the drapery as if there was something of importance she needed to see. But Richard knew this was just another ploy to keep him in her presence longer. "I would think you would know why I'm here, my love. I want to win you back. I knew if I could just see you again, I could convince you we belong together," she replied with a wave of her hand.

"I can't believe you actually think showing up at a Society ball would suddenly change my mind," he growled before pinching the bridge of his nose in frustration.

"Why not? Cannot I rival any woman who is below?" Her eyes narrowed before she once more came forward. "Unless..."

"Unless, what?"

She inspected her nails for a moment before she took hold of his jacket and pulled bringing them chest to chest. She yanked so hard, he steadied himself by grabbing hold of her waist. "Unless you think that young little miss you were dancing with could actually replace me? As if anyone could take my place in your heart." She wound her arm around his neck and gave him a coy smile.

"Richard?" A voice from the doorway broke them apart, but it was the stricken look in Patience's eyes that was Richard's undoing.

"Oh, there is the dear child now," Penelope sneered in contempt.

"Shut up, Penelope," Richard warned, but it was no use. Penelope was here for revenge, and she apparently wanted to take it out on the innocent woman with tears running down her cheeks.

"Who is this woman, Richard?" Patience asked with a trembling voice.

"No one," he replied before a shrill snigger left Penelope.

Penelope's eyes narrowed when she returned her attention to him. "Really, Richard? I've been *someone* for many years and you know it. Tell this lady who I am."

The color drained from Patience's face and he could not erase the betrayal that flashed in her eyes. "You may address me as Countess Seahaven," she said angrily. Her chin rose in defiance.

"Countess? Richard, you really are moving up in the world. What would a countess ever want with a mere viscount? It just isn't done, my dear."

"I told you to shut up, Penelope," he snapped, but that was when the woman drove her dagger home, aimed directly at Patience's tender heart.

"You have a lot to learn in the ways of men if you think he would ever propose to you, my lady. Richard is more of a rake than husband material. I should know, having been in his bed for the past several years."

A sob escaped Patience and she stumbled backwards in disbelief. Their eyes met briefly before she quickly turned and fled down the hall. With no further thoughts of Penelope, he ran to follow Patience, but he was too late when she ran into a room, slammed the door, and the lock clicked into place.

"Patience! Open the door," he demanded without success.

"Leave me alone, Richard," she cried out. "I never want to see you again."

"Please listen to reason," he attempted again resting his forehead on the wooden door that kept him from the woman who owned his heart.

"I have nothing to say to you."

He knew she had moved deeper into the room only because her crying sounded farther away. He swore, knowing there was nothing he could do to redeem himself if the lady wouldn't give him a minute to explain.

He returned downstairs to find Penelope waiting for him.

"Upset with you, is she? How will she feel when she sees me again and again around town? Do you think she will forgive you?"

"Why are you doing this, Penelope? You know it is over between us. What do you want from me? Because I will tell you now, if you hurt Lady Seahaven, I will make sure you live to regret it."

"Give me one thousand pounds, and I will go away," Penelope replied, without hesitation. "I have a chance in America, a man who will marry me, but we need a nest egg to make a fresh start." She tossed her head as though she knew she would get what she desired from him if it meant she would be out of his life for good.

"So, you decided to put on this little display to force my hand? You would have been better to ask me. I might have given you additional money for old time's sake. Have I ever treated you unfairly?" His voice rose when his anger got the better of him.

"That is hardly the point, Richard," she said. "I just need—"

"Go away, Penelope. I never want to see you again. If you've already gone through the settlement I left you, then that's your problem. You'll get nothing more from me." He left her in the entryway sputtering her displeasure.

Richard fumed at the gall of his ex-mistress, but he could not change the damage she had done. There was nothing to keep his interest in the ball now that Patience was no longer in attendance. His sister noticed him by the doorway to the ballroom and made her way to him.

"Can we go home?" she asked, a worried frown marred her brow. She appeared as if she was on the verge of tears.

"What's happened?" God forbid another catastrophe was in the making.

"I just want to leave. Is there anything wrong with that?"

"We're at a ball, and you were enjoying yourself, earlier. If I recall, you were happily dancing with Milton. Where is he?"

"Who cares! I want to go home, Richard. Now." Her raised voice caused several nearby couples to turn in their direction.

He watched her suspiciously wondering what happened. "Do I need to call Milton out?"

Her eyes widened before tears pooled in their

depths. "No. We had a falling out. Now, can you please take me home?"

"Of course." He took her arm and escorted her from the Assembly room.

But as their carriage was brought around, he swore he caught the briefest glimpse of Patience staring at him from one of the upper windows. How was he ever going to make this up to her when Penelope had ruined an evening for Patience that should have been a happy memory?

CHAPTER 14

I n all things that *really* mattered, her daughters, the ball had been a great success. For days, flowers and invitations had been sent to the town house until you couldn't enter any one particular room without the smell of one floral arrangement after another. Patience was happy for them, truly she was, and yet for her the ball had become a grim reminder that love would seemingly pass her by.

She could relive that horrid moment a thousand times, and everything would still be filled with the shock of it all. She had sworn time had stood still as she swayed on her feet at the audacity of the woman who apparently had been Richard's mistress. The fact the woman had showed up uninvited at *her* ball, only fueled her anger. Well... only after a lot of fallen tears.

But facts were facts, at least as far as Patience and her

broken heart was concerned. Her world had turned upside down the moment she decided to follow Richard up those blasted stairs. A dark sickening grief had consumed her seeing another woman in his arms. Yet in many ways, perhaps this was for the best. She would be feeling more hurt than she was now if she had given herself to him that night at his town house. His betrayal would have then stung far worse than the bitterness now surrounding her heart leaving her feeling completely empty.

She had refused to see him even though Barbara and Doro told her to hear him out. They had been supportive when Patience confided in them and it had meant the world to her. But she still couldn't do it. She needed time to process what had happened and eventually she would most likely see for herself a vengeful woman who only meant to hurt a man by any means possible. Clearly the female wanted him back.

If she thought about it hard enough, she would forgive him instead of letting that woman unknowingly win by splitting them apart. So why couldn't she face Richard? Patience didn't have any answer. Consumed with self-pity and unable to take that first step toward reconciliation, she did the one thing to take her mind off her troubles. She baked.

Kneading the dough became a sort of therapy while she took out her frustrations by punching the ball over and over again before breaking it down into individual loaves to rise. She hadn't realized she had made so much until she ran out of tins to bake them in. They would never eat it all before it spoiled.

She decided to take the extra loaves to a local merchant who had been friends with her mother and father. Upon their arrival in York, this woman had recognized Patience, assured her that her secret was safe, but also said that if Patience inherited her parents' skill, the merchant would be willing to sell any baked items she could supply.

Which brought Patience back to the present, walking down a fourteenth-century cobblestone street in an area called The Shambles. The hood of her cape thrown over her head, she held her basket covered in a towel in front of her like a shield while making her way through this seedier side of town. She kept her head low in her attempt to not draw attention to herself until she looked up to get her bearings. A gasp escaped her when she immediately saw Richard riding a white horse.

Their eyes met, and a scowl crossed his features before he put his heel to the horse's side to pick up the pace to get to her quickly. She panicked and ran in the opposite direction, quickly ducking into an alleyway. Her back to the stone building, her chest heaved in an attempt to fill her lungs with much needed air. Her day had been bad enough, but it was about to get a whole lot worse.

" Eeup, look at this, lads. She's a fine un." A crude voice echoed between the buildings, and Patience gulped when several men stepped forward.

"A real lady, she be," another said.

"Naw! No lady would be showin' her face on this side of town." He smacked his lips before drawing closer inspecting her from head to toe. "How much for a tumble, girlie?"

She was trapped. Hands began to claw at her. "Get off me!" she hissed attempting to use the basket as some sort of useless weapon.

"Maybe she likes it rough," the first man grinned with her efforts to slap their hands away as the basket went flying.

"Who wants a go at her first?"

Her mind racing and eyes wide in fright, she screamed out for the only person who could save her. "*Richard!*"

"That's not me name, but thee can call me anything thee wish, doll." One came closer, reaching beneath her cloak to tear at the bodice of her gown. She let out another blood curdling scream while they all came at her at once. A gunshot exploded into the air, and the men stopped their attempts to ravage her.

Richard sat on his horse carefully reloading his pistol before he aimed it at her tormentors. "Put one more hand on the lady and the next bullet won't be in the air."

The men scattered like ants, leaving Patience mortified at what almost happened to her. Pulling her cloak around her to cover her ruined gown, she chanced a glance at the man who had come to her rescue like a knight in shining armor... white horse and all!

He dismounted, and yet his displeasure at seeing her in such condition only made things worse.

"What the bloody hell are you doing in this part of town, Patience?" he growled at her like some wounded animal.

She sucked in a sharp breath of disbelief at the nerve of him to chastise her after what almost happened to her. "I was almost attacked and you're going to berate me while going about an errand?"

"Yes!" he fumed. "That's what servants are for."

She straightened her posture to glare at him. "As you may, or may not be aware or perhaps forgot, I have limited staff to run my household. Not that it's any of your business." She looked around on the ground to see her basket, the loaves of bread now useless as they were strewn in every direction. She picked up the wicker hamper and made to whisk past him. He grabbed her arm, halting her progress to leave.

"Where do you think you're going?" he demanded while drawing in slow steady breaths as if to calm his unsuppressed anger.

"Where do you think? I'm going home!"

"Not without an escort."

"I don't need you to take me home, Richard." Her voice betrayed her as did her heart while he continued to hold her arm.

He guided her to his horse before cupping his hands

to help her mount. She stood staring at him as if he had lost his mind. They couldn't be seen together on a horse!

She shook her head. "I don't think so."

His head cocked to one side before his eyes widened apparently in disbelief she would dare to disobey him. "Get on the damn horse, Patience."

Her chin rose defiantly. "No."

He swore before taking her about the waist and lifting her into the saddle. He put his foot in the stirrup and swung up behind her. The feel of the entire length of his firm muscular body against her back made her stiffen.

"What are you doing?" she barely managed to whisper when he reached around her to take up the leather reins.

"What does it look like? I'm taking you home and I don't want to hear another word of protest from those beautiful lips of yours," he warned, but the softer tone caused a moment of pleasure to rush through her. He could in no way conceal his concern for her welfare.

Before she could make any sort of protest, he kicked his heels into the horse's side and the steed took off in a trot. Every bump brought her into his hard chest reminding her of what she had almost had. Love... if only she had given it a further chance to bloom.

They rode in silence for several minutes before his gentle voice finally spoke. "Are you hurt?"

It took her a few minutes to decide on how to

answer him, knowing if anything she needed to offer her gratitude from saving her from the worse possible situation a woman could find herself in. "From what those men did? Nothing that can't be repaired. Thank you for coming to my aid."

"You're welcome." He pulled on the reins bringing her closer when a dog ran in front of the horse. "And the other night? Will you let me explain?"

She nervously bit her lip before slightly turning her head, so she could glance into his face. She could see for herself the anguish he attempted to conceal, hidden just beneath the surface. She had asked this of him once... she would need to ask him for what she needed again. "I need time, Richard."

He nodded his head, and she returned her attention to what lay before them. "Take all the time you need, Patience. I'm not going anywhere."

He may not be going anywhere, but Patience knew her time in York was coming to an end. Still, his vow filled her heart with possibilities. Yet there was still some small bit inside her that wasn't sure if she could trust him. If he could give her time, then she would take what he offered in order for her heart to mend.

CHAPTER 15

Richard's carriage made its way through the muddy streets of Starbrook. The rain continued to pour down from the skies and mirrored his mood of late. He knew he had told Patience he would give her all the time she needed to overcome the diabolical fiasco Penelope created, but how could he make amends if the woman he loved was no longer in York?

April had turned into May. Penelope must have taken him seriously, because he didn't see her again. Other than when he rescued the countess, he didn't see her, either, except for one day at the races. He wanted to run to her side, but when he happened to catch her glance, a simple shake of her head told him more than any words she could have spoken. She still wasn't ready.

With the Season over, even Josephine's chances of finding a match had dwindled to nothing giving Richard the impression she cared more for his friend Milton than she let on. He would need to talk to him and soon. In the meantime, he had made arrangements for his cousin to return to London with them and Josephine would now reside under his roof. There was no way he would allow his sister to remain in the toxic environment revolving around their parents.

Which brought him back to his mission to see Patience after Josephine all but begged him to seek the lady out. It could be a mistake, but he was tired of waiting. He needed an answer as to her feelings for him. If she wished to no longer see him, then so be it. He would move on... as if he could.

The carriage left the village and the driver soon pulled up to a two-story cottage that had seen better days. Even with the rain pelting down, it was hard to imagine what didn't need to be repaired with the place Patience called home. He hated to think what the cottage appeared like on a sunny day. He let himself out before the footman could put the step down and quickly ran up the walkway to raise the knocker.

Lady Emma opened the door before he had the chance to knock a second time. Her bright smile welcomed him into her home. "I'm so pleased you are here, Lord Cranfield," she said waving him inside. A puddle formed beneath his feet confirming how hard it was raining before a woman he assumed was their housekeeper came and took his hat and coat.

"Is your mother available?" he asked. He raised his eyes as two of Patience's stepdaughters were poised on the stairs along with another who came from the front parlor with her gentleman caller. Shock at seeing him here was mirrored on their faces.

"Perhaps you can talk some sense into mama," Emma exclaimed with a heavy sigh.

"Emma!" Several of the sisters said her name at the same time before she gave them all a stern look and stomped her foot. For a twelve-year old it was something to behold.

"Someone needs to, and she refuses to listen to any of us," she argued tugging on his arm.

"Where is she?" he inquired as he followed her toward the back of the cottage.

"Standing in the middle of our garden. I suppose we should ask Mrs. Crewe to return your hat and coat before you go back out into the rain."

"Don't bother. How long has she been outside?" He shook his head sadly.

"Seems like hours," Emma sadly replied. "You will convince her to come inside, won't you, my lord?"

He looked down into the young girl's green eyes and gave her a convincing smile. "I will."

Satisfied, Emma nodded and pointed to the door. "You'll find her out there."

Richard didn't hesitate and opened the door Emma had pointed to. Patience's stepdaughter wasn't wrong. The countess stood in the middle of the garden soaking wet, and he could see her shivering from here. Eyes closed, her head was bent back as if the heavens held all her answers, but none were forthcoming. He took several steps forward before he stopped not knowing if he would be welcome or not.

"Patience." Her name escaped his lips with a yearning he had been holding inside for a month since he had last spoken to her. Her head came forward and she gave a heavy sigh before she opened her blue-grey eyes and turned slightly towards him.

"Richard." The sound of his name filled the missing void that had been barely holding him together. He took another step closer, pulled off his jacket, and placed the garment around her shoulders.

"What are you doing standing out here in the rain?" he asked quietly before extending his hand wondering if she would take it. When her cold fingertips traced his own, he took hold of them bringing them to his lips.

"Pondering life's mysteries?" she declared teasingly.

Her red-rimmed eyes couldn't mask the fact she was upset. "You've been crying."

She offered him a slight tilt of a smile before she lowered her eyes nodding towards the cottage. "They can't see my tears out here in the rain," she confessed. "I never expected to see you in Starbrook, Richard."

"I hope you're glad I'm here," he said waiting hopefully for her reply.

She turned to face him. "I am."

"Patience, I can't tell you how sorry I am about what happened at the ball," he began before she placed her fingertips on his lips to silence him.

"And I am sorry I didn't give you time to explain while I was still in York. I suppose it was silly of me. Here I am, a countess, and you would think I would be more worldly and handle things differently when a vengeful woman wants to claim she holds the heart of a man who clearly wants nothing to do with her." Her smile reached her eyes, and he was thankful she had come to her own conclusion.

"I never loved Penelope, and she never loved me, Patience. She pulled that stunt wanting more money than I had already given her when I ended our agreement before I ever came to York. There is only one woman who has ever held my heart, Patience, and that lady is you."

She nodded as the droplets of water continued to rain down upon them. "And you have owned mine from the very moment we touched. I never thought love at first sight could happen until it happened with you. I thought I had lost you through my foolishness in not letting you explain."

"You never lost me, Patience. You asked for time, and I could do nothing else but give you whatever time you needed to decide our fate. But I couldn't stay away any longer, and this is why I'm standing here with you now."

"You never gave up on me," she murmured looking at him with hopeful eyes.

"Never!" He brought her into his arms and leaned

down to press his forehead onto hers. "Can you forgive me so we might start again?"

"Only if you can forgive me for not giving you a chance to explain the situation yourself."

"I never want anything to come between us again. Forgive me," he insisted taking her hand and placing a kiss on the inside of her wrist.

Her free hand cupped his cheek. "Richard... surely you know there is nothing to forgive. I love you, and I hope you can—

"I love you too, Patience," he finished before bending down to seal their love with a kiss. It was shorter than he would have liked, but he could feel Patience trembling from the cold. "Now, let's get you inside before you become ill."

He hugged her to him, and as they turned toward the cottage, the windows were filled with the smiling faces of her stepdaughters. Patience waved, and they returned her gesture. Laughter escaped her, and he chuckled as well to join in her merriment.

Patience would always be his countess to remember for the rest of his days. He had found the love of a good woman, and now he knew that love was returned. And as he walked toward his future with Patience at his side, he knew that she and her daughters would all become the family he had always wanted. Life with her was going to be heavenly, and Richard would do anything to ensure she never wanted for anything but the love they had found together.

EPILOGUE

London, England
One Year Later

Her London house was filled to the brim with family and friends who had come to see the new baby held lovingly in Patience's arms and to witness the baptism. She only wished her parents yet lived to see their second grandchild. Richard, bless his heart, had seen to the much-needed repairs to the cottage, and it now appeared how Patience remembered it from her youth.

Her gaze travelled around the room, and a smile swept her face while she fondly looked upon her step-daughters and the gentlemen they had fallen in love with. Happiness filled Patience's heart with joy with the knowledge that they, too, had found men who were worthy of them. York had certainly been a magnificent success, for they had all found their hearts desire and a love to last them a lifetime.

Richard's friends stood in a corner grouped together with a glass of brandy in their hands. Two were married and their wives, Lady Beacham and Lady Osgood gave winks of conspiracy to the remaining bachelors in the group. Patience had learned from Richard the women were on a mission to see them all wed. Patience had no doubt they would succeed.

Patience had taken on the title of Viscountess after a heated discussion with her at the time soon-to-be husband. He thought she should keep her original title, but the title of countess never meant as much to her as did taking on Richard's title. Love... it explained so much and could change everything. He had stopped arguing his point, but Patience knew he was happy with her decision. They had quietly married with their family and friends in attendance last year.

The whispering between Emma and Merry grew louder before Emma gave her sister a nudge. Merry got up off the floor and came over to her mother. Peering at the infant snuggled in a blue blanket fast asleep, she wrinkled her nose. "Whatever are we to do with a *boy*, Mama?"

The room became silent before everyone began to laugh. Patience put her free arm around her stepdaughter. "We will love him just as much as we love one another, sweetling."

"But he's a boy, Mama," she repeated, clearly not

impressed at her new sibling. "He's not going to want to play dolls with us."

Richard, who sat in a chair on the other side of his wife, choked back his amusement and covered his mouth with his hand. Merry turned her face toward him. "I am certain we will think of something we can all do together when he gets older... as a family."

"If you say so, Papa," Merry replied with a shrug. She went back to sit on the floor with Emma and Jane to take up the dolls they had been playing with.

Patience gazed up at her husband. "Good answer."

He kissed her forehead before taking a finger to slightly pull the blanket to look more closely at his child. "Have I told you thank you for our son, my love?" he whispered in her ear causing Patience to shiver in delight.

"Many times, my lord," she returned with a brilliant smile. A yawn suddenly escaped her, and her eyes widened. "Oh dear, I guess I'm more tired than I thought."

Lady Osgood stepped forward. "Here... let me take him. It's been a while since I've held a little one."

Patience handed her son over. "Thank you, Lady Osgood."

"You must call me Constance. After all, our men are good friends, and I know we shall become the same," she replied before taking the baby over to Lady Beacham, who Patience knew would also ask her to call her by her given name, Margaret.

Richard helped her rise from the chair and gave their excuses so he could see Patience to their room for a much-needed nap. He waved off her maid, telling the girl he would see to his wife's needs before closing their bedroom door. With her gown removed, he pulled back the covers and tucked Patience inside. She gave a heavenly sigh, but as he turned to leave she tugged at his hand.

"Stay with me until I fall asleep," she urged.

He lay down beside her on top of the covers knowing he had guests to see to. Still, he pulled her close to him. "I love you, my darling wife."

"As I love you, my dearest husband," she replied before she gave another yawn.

"Watch for me in your dreams," he whispered before kissing the back of her head.

"I always dream of you... my handsome knight who came to my rescue," Patience replied before closing her eyes.

His arms held her closely and happiness once again swelled around her heart and soul. Yes... Richard had rescued them all in more ways than Patience could ever imagine. Love had found her at first sight, and she was grateful to the man who fulfilled all of her wildest dreams. They had a bright future to look forward to, and she couldn't wait to see what their lives together could bring. She was dearly loved, along with her daughters, and life with Richard and her family had made her complete.

THE END

***

Sherry Ewing needs your help!
Book reviews help readers to find books, and authors to find readers. Please consider writing a review for **_A Countess to Remember_**, even a couple of sentences telling people what you liked (or didn't like) about the story is helpful. Reviews can be posted on BookBub, Goodreads, and on most eRetailer websites. For links to this book on those sites, see my website at www. sherryewing.com/books

AUTHOR'S NOTE

Richard Cranfield made his first appearance as a secondary character in my Regency novellas, *Under the Mistletoe* and *A Second Chance at Love*. Now it was time for him to get his happily-ever-after story and Patience, Lady Seahaven was just the heroine he needed. I look forward to writing Milton's and George's stories in the future. You can learn more about my other Regency, medieval, and time travel stories on my website at https://www.sherryewing.com/books.

Medieval & Time Travel Series

To Love A Scottish Laird: De Wolfe Pack Connected World

Sometimes you really can fall in love at first sight...

To Love An English Knight: De Wolfe Pack Connected World

Can a chance encounter lead to love?

If My Heart Could See You: The MacLarens, A Medieval Romance (Book One)

When you're enemies, does love have a fighting chance?

For All of Ever: The Knights of Berwyck, A Quest Through Time (Book One)

Sometimes to find your future, you must look to the past...

Only For You: The Knights of Berwyck, A Quest Through Time (Book Two)

Sometimes it's hard to remember that true love conquers all, only after the battle is over...

Hearts Across Time: The Knights of Berwyck (Books One & Two)

Sometimes all you need is to just believe... Hearts Across Time is a special edition box set that combines Katherine and Riorden's stories together from *For All of Ever* and *Only For You*.

A Knight To Call My Own: The MacLarens, A Medieval Romance (Book Two)

When your heart is broken, is love still worth the risk?

To Follow My Heart: The Knights of Berwyck, A Quest Through Time (Book Three)

Love is a leap. Sometimes you need to jump...

The Piper's Lady: The MacLarens, A Medieval Romance (Book Three)

True love binds them. Deceit divides them. Will they choose love?

Love Will Find You: The Knights of Berwyck, A Quest Through Time (Book Four)

Sometimes a moment is all we have...

One Last Kiss: The Knights of Berwyck, A Quest Through Time (Book Five)

Sometimes it takes a miracle to find your heart's desire...

Promises Made At Midnight: The Knights of Berwyck, A Quest Through Time (Book Six)

Make a wish...

Regency

A Kiss For Charity: A de Courtenay Novella (Book One)

Love heals all wounds but will their pride keep them apart?

The Earl Takes A Wife: A de Courtenay Novella (Book Two)

It began with a memory, etched in the heart.

Before I Found You: A de Courtenay Novella (Book Three)

A quest for a title. An encounter with a stranger. Will she choose love?

Nothing But Time: A Family of Worth (Book One)

They will risk everything for their forbidden love...

One Moment In Time: A Family of Worth (Book Two)

One moment in time may be enough, if it lasts forever...

Under the Mistletoe

A new suitor seeks her hand. An old flame holds her heart. Which one will she meet under the kissing bough?

A Second Chance At Love

Can the bittersweet frost of lost love be rekindled into a burning flame?

A Countess to Remember

Sometimes love finds you when you least expect it...

You can find out more about Sherry's work on her website at www.SherryEwing.com and at online retailers.

SOCIAL MEDIA

Website: www.SherryEwing.com
Email: Sherry@SherryEwing.com
Bluestocking Belles: www.bluestockingbelles.net/
Amazon Author Page: http://amzn.to/1TrWtoy
Bookbub: www.bookbub.com/authors/sherry-ewing
Facebook: www.Facebook.com/SherryEwingAuthor
Goodreads: www.Goodreads.com/author/show/8382315.
Sherry_Ewing
Instagram: https://instagram.com/sherry.ewing
Pinterest: www.Pinterest.com/SherryLEwing
TikTok: https://www.tiktok.com/@sherryewingauthor
Tumblr: https://sherryewing.tumblr.com
Twitter: www.Twitter.com/Sherry_Ewing
YouTube: http://www.youtube.com/SherryEwingauthor

Sign Me Up!
Newsletter: http://bit.ly/2vGrqQM
Facebook Street Team:
www.facebook.com/groups/799623313455472/
Facebook Official Fan page: https://www.facebook.com/
groups/356905935241836/

ABOUT SHERRY EWING

Sherry Ewing picked up her first historical romance when she was a teenager and has been hooked ever since. A bestselling and award winning author, she writes historical and time travel romances to awaken the soul one heart at a time. When not writing, she can be found in the San Francisco area at her day job as an Information Technology Specialist. You can learn more about Sherry on her website where a new adventure awaits you on every page.

Learn more about Sherry at:
Email: Sherry@SherryEwing.com
Newsletter: http://bit.ly/2vGrqQM
Facebook Street Team: https://www.facebook.com/
groups/799623313455472/
Facebook Official Fan page: https://www.facebook.com/
groups/356905935241836/

Printed in Great Britain
by Amazon

19639150R00082